MW01269104

DEADLY

FALLOUT

RED STONE SECURITY SERIES

Katie Reus

Copyright © 2014 by Katie Reus

All rights reserved. Except as permitted under the U.S. Copyright Act of 1976, no part of this publication may be reproduced, distributed, or transmitted in any form or by any means, or stored in a database or retrieval system, without the prior written permission of the author. Thank you for buying an authorized version of this book and complying with copyright laws. You're supporting writers and encouraging creativity.

Cover art: Jaycee of Sweet 'N Spicy Designs
JRT Editing
Book Layout ©2013 BookDesignTemplates.com

Author website: http://www.katiereus.com

Publisher's Note: This is a work of fiction. Names, characters, places, and incidents are either the products of the author's imagination or used fictitiously, and any resemblance to actual persons, living or dead, or business establishments, organizations or locales is completely coincidental.

Deadly Fallout/Katie Reus. -- 1st ed.

ISBN-13: 9781503032880
ISBN-10: 1503032884

eISBN: 9781942447009

Ten books in and the Red Stone Security series is still going strong because of you, my wonderful readers. Thank you.

Praise for the novels of Katie Reus

"…an engrossing page-turner that I enjoyed in one sitting. Reus offers all the ingredients I love in a paranormal romance."
—Book Lovers, Inc.

"Has all the right ingredients: a hot couple, evil villains, and a killer action-filled plot. . . . [The] Moon Shifter series is what I call Grade-A entertainment!" —Joyfully Reviewed

"I could not put this book down. . . . Let me be clear that I am not saying that this was a good book *for* a paranormal genre; it was an excellent romance read, *period*." —All About Romance

"Reus strikes just the right balance of steamy sexual tension and nail-biting action….This romantic thriller reliably hits every note that fans of the genre will expect." —*Publishers Weekly*

"Prepare yourself for the start of a great new series! . . . I'm excited about reading more about this great group of characters."
—Fresh Fiction

"Wow! This powerful, passionate hero sizzles with sheer deliciousness. I loved every sexy twist of this fun & exhilarating tale. Katie Reus delivers!" —Carolyn Crane, RITA award winning author

Continued…

"You'll fall in love with Katie's heroes."
—*New York Times* bestselling author, Kaylea Cross

"A sexy, well-crafted paranormal romance that succeeds with smart characters and creative world building."—Kirkus Reviews

"*Mating Instinct*'s romance is taut and passionate . . . Katie Reus's newest installment in her Moon Shifter series will leave readers breathless!" —Stephanie Tyler, *New York Times* bestselling author

"Reus has definitely hit a home run with this series. . . . This book has mystery, suspense, and a heart-pounding romance that will leave you wanting more." —Nocturne Romance Reads

"Katie Reus pulls the reader into a story line of second chances, betrayal, and the truth about forgotten lives and hidden pasts."
—The Reading Café

"If you are looking for a really good, new military romance series, pick up *Targeted*! The new Deadly Ops series stands to be a passionate and action-riddled read."
—That's What I'm Talking About

"Sexy suspense at its finest." —Laura Wright, *New York Times* bestselling author of *Branded*

Zoe Hansen slipped her earbuds into her ears, the soft classical music drowning out the typical hospital sounds as she stepped out of the elevator. It was four in the morning and time for her required break from the ER rush since she was working a double.

Normally she took her breaks with friends, but this morning, she actually needed some alone time. One of her fellow surgeons had been harassing her lately. Subtle stuff at first; innuendos in front of co-workers, trying to make it sound like they were a couple.

Please.

First of all, the guy was married so there was no way in hell she'd ever date or sleep with him. And second, he was twenty years older than her and definitely not her type. The age thing actually didn't bother her much, it was his douchey personality and God complex.

But tonight things had gotten even weirder. He'd sent her two dozen red roses and made a point to ask her about them in front of some of her co-workers. It had been incredibly embarrassing and unprofessional. She needed to decompress and go over her options because she wasn't letting this crap continue any longer.

As soon as her shift was over, she was talking to someone in the HR department. She understood the annoying politics of the hospital and that she shouldn't 'make waves' but she'd never put up with anyone's crap and wasn't about to start now. Especially not with this kind of creepy behavior.

When she reached a room she knew was often un-used, she ducked inside. After checking the bathroom to make sure it really was empty, she flipped the lights off, letting the illumination from outside the two big win-dows guide her. Sighing in relief, she eyed the bed and the bench by the window. If she got in the bed she'd pass out and her break was too short for a real nap. Heading to the window, she stretched out on the padded cushion and leaned her head back against the wall. Since she was petite she didn't have to scrunch her legs too much.

Before she closed her eyes, she set her phone alarm to go off in twenty-five minutes. The buzzing would jar her awake if for some reason she dozed off.

"Finally, peace," she murmured to the empty room. The bright city lights of Miami weren't even a distrac-tion as she let her eyes close. She'd had so many back-to-back surgeries yesterday and early this morning that nothing could distract her now.

Sweet rest edged her consciousness as the soft music helped calm her frayed nerves. When she felt her phone buzzing in her pocket, she shifted against the seat. Had she actually fallen asleep? Opening her eyes, she fished into her pocket and looked at her screen—and sighed. Only a couple minutes had passed but there was an emergency. Of course. That's what she got for trying to sneak away for a few minutes.

As she swung her legs off the bench, a slight movement in the shadows on the other side of the bed made her freeze. Heart pounding, she pulled her earbuds out. Holding her breath, she paused, listening and watching.

A curtain had been pulled back from the uncovered bed, but she could swear she saw movement. Or maybe it was her imagination going crazy because she'd been so tense lately. She'd felt as if she was being watched, possibly even followed.

Squeak.

Shit. Blood rushed in her ears. "Who's there?" she demanded, glad her voice came out strong. This floor wasn't as busy as the ER but it wasn't devoid of people. It was too damn dark to see behind the curtain. With no light from the bathroom behind it, it was like a dark abyss.

When Braddock Klein stepped out of the shadows, ice flooded her veins. Him being here after his weird behavior lately was *not* good. "I'm glad you could sneak away so we could spend time together," he murmured, his voice low and probably what he thought of as seductive.

Sneak away? Her heart rate kicked up again, the staccato beat going overtime. "What are you talking about?" She kept her voice even as she took a step away from the bench. She tried to keep her movements small, not wanting to give away that she was trying to make it to the door.

He was in street clothes, dark slacks and a business casual Polo shirt. He was tall and dark-haired, with a distinguished face. In his fifties, he was a handsome-looking man in a country club, preppy sort of way. Or he would be if it wasn't for the fact that he was clearly deranged.

"I know you come up here sometimes," he said, moving to the end of the bed and effectively blocking her escape.

Almost no one knew she used this room for downtime so he had to have been watching her *closely*. Zoe took a step away from him and toward a rolling cart. It was in the opposite direction of the door, but she needed a weapon if things escalated. Because the look in his eyes was creepy as hell and she wasn't ignoring her instincts.

"Why are you here?" Her voice shook.

His head tilted to the side a fraction and he looked at her as if her question was stupid. "You know why. I don't understand why you keep playing so hard to get. Everyone here already thinks we're a couple."

"You're married," she said, even though that wasn't remotely the point. She just wanted to get his focus back on reality.

Klein made a weird tsking sound and stepped closer, rounding the bed now. "You're mine, Zoe," he growled, his face turning feral as he lunged for her.

Zoe dove for the rolling cart and grabbed a metal bedpan on the bottom shelf. She'd barely grasped it in her fingers when Klein tackled her to the bed, his big body pinning her face-down. The pan fell to the floor with a clatter.

She slammed her head back, trying to break his nose, but he twisted to the side, avoiding what would have been a hard blow.

"Bitch," he snarled.

She let a scream rip free as she tried to scramble over the bed. The door was so close, just within her grasp. Her feet hit the floor but before she'd taken two steps he tackled her again, slamming her against the wall and cutting short her cries for help.

The pain jarring her entire body barely registered as he hissed in her ear, his breath hot as it rushed over her skin. "You're going to learn your place." His thick arm wrapped around her neck as he tugged her back against him.

Struggling to breathe, she clutched his arm as he lifted her off the ground. Oh God, she couldn't breathe!

His hand clawed at her crotch over her scrubs. Tears stung her eyes at the violation. She kicked back with one of her feet, barely clipping his shin—

The door opened and lights flooded the room.

Instantly he dropped her. Without thinking Zoe sprinted for the door. A female janitor looked at her in surprise as she rounded the small entryway. The cleaning cart blocked Zoe. On instinct, she turned back toward Klein, ready to defend herself. But he just stood there, adjusting his shirt, tucking it into his pants. Except for his ruffled hair, he looked completely unaffected.

"Is everything okay?" the woman asked.

Zoe shook her head. "No. Come on." She shoved at the cart and forced the woman back into the hall. She didn't care how rude she was being, she needed to get the hell out of the room and away from him. As they spilled out into the hallway, she pointed toward the elevators. "Get off this floor now." She didn't have time to explain herself to the woman and Zoe wanted her out of harm's way.

As the woman hurried in the other direction, Zoe raced for the nearest nurses' station to get help. She risked a glance over her shoulder as she ran and saw Klein strolling out of the room. He was smoothing his dark hair into place, his movements unhurried.

Fear battled with outrage inside her when he winked—actually winked—and turned away from her, heading toward the elevators as if he didn't have a care in the world.

CHAPTER ONE

Seven months later

"You about out of here?"

Zoe looked up at the sound of her new boss, Gerard Fernandez's voice. "Yes. Seriously, I can't believe I didn't know how great private practice could be." After leaving the public hospital months ago she hadn't realized what a toll the hours and stress had been taking on her personal life. Now she left work every day between five and six, could actually take days off and had her own office. She grabbed her jacket off the back of her leather rolling chair and slipped it on as she rounded the desk.

A grin tugged at his mouth. "You're preaching to the choir. Come on, we're the last two here. I'll walk you to your car."

"You don't have to." Gerard knew what had happened to her at the hospital and Klein's subsequent threats, but that wasn't why he was walking her to her car. He walked every woman who worked at his family practice to her car when they got off work. He was like a throwback to a different era. Just one of those truly good men she was glad to call her friend.

He simply snorted. "That line's getting old, Hansen. Besides, isn't *he* . . . getting back in town soon?"

Throat tight, Zoe nodded and found her voice. Her gaze automatically went to the wall calendar, as if she didn't know the exact day that freak show Braddock Klein was returning from his six month Medicine Without Borders stint overseas. "Yeah."

"You told your family yet?" he asked as she turned her lights off and stepped out into the hall with him.

Zoe scowled. "Remind me again why I told you about all this?"

He just snorted again because they both knew the answer. After Klein's attack, the whole thing had turned into a he-said, she-said type of situation. And since the psycho had been—unbeknownst to her—laying the groundwork at work so that everyone thought she was in some type of relationship with him, her work life had basically imploded. Apparently it was much easier for her co-workers to believe that she was just some slut hooking up with a married doctor and had then decided to press charges against him for 'fill in the blank'. She'd heard all the rumors after everything had gone down and they'd all horrified her. He'd refused to leave his wife for her, so she'd decided to cry would-be rape. It shouldn't shock her so much that people she'd worked with hadn't seen the truth, but it did. At least she'd been able to get a temporary restraining order against him—

unfortunately permanent ones were almost impossible to get.

Of course hindsight sucked. There were signs that something had been wrong with Klein, but it had all been little stuff. Unfortunately it all added up to a grade A psychopath who'd become insanely focused on her.

And now said psychopath was returning to the States in a week. "I'm scared," she finally said into the quiet as they strode down the hallway that led to the door that emptied into the waiting room. They always left out the front door after dark because there was better lighting.

"You've taken all the right precautions, but you need to tell your family," he said as they strode through the small waiting room and into the lobby.

It was already dark outside, the lights from the parking lot bright through the wall of windows. "I know. I will." But she hated the thought of worrying them. Her brother was now blissfully engaged, her two sisters had busy lives and big families, and her mom would just worry. It didn't matter that she and her mom butted heads more often than not, Zoe didn't like upsetting her mom. And Klein had left the country months ago so there'd been no reason to make her mom worry needlessly. Especially when there was nothing she could do about it.

Gerard shook his head and made a disapproving sound, likely because he'd heard this before. She really was going to tell them, it was just . . . hell, if she said it out loud, it became real. This whole, horrible situation became real. Not to mention that if she admitted it, it almost made her feel weak. Like she was admitting that she'd become a victim in this mess.

Sighing, she nudged the glass door open with her hip and shoved her hands in her jacket pockets. Her phone and keys were in one and the pepper spray she always carried now was in the other. She'd actually gotten a concealed weapon permit but simply couldn't carry a gun around. It felt too weird. The chilly December air rolled over her, reminding her that she still needed to buy Christmas presents for her huge family. Of course her put-together sisters would have already done their shopping months ago. Not Zoe, she saved everything until the last minute. It worked for her.

Gerard began locking up the exterior glass door. She knew from watching him do it a hundred times that he would set the alarm remotely once the building was locked up tight. Instinctively, she scanned the parking lot—and froze when she saw Klein leaning against the back of her two-door car. *No.* Her throat tightened as fear scraped across her skin.

"Gerard," she rasped out, wondering if she'd lost her mind and was now seeing things.

She heard the snicking of the deadbolt sliding into place before he said, "What's..." Suddenly Gerard was standing in front of her, moving incredibly fast as he started striding across the parking lot with determination.

That was the only thing that moved her into action; seeing her boss taking action. Because the truth was, the sight of Klein terrified her. She'd always been so sure of who she was and what she wanted to do with her life. From the time she'd been a kid she'd wanted to be a doctor and no matter what, with everything else going on in her life, the hospital had always been her safe haven. She'd loved it there—and he'd taken that feeling of security from her.

No more.

Gripping her pepper spray tight, she pulled her hand out of her pocket and hurried to catch up with Gerard. Her boots clicked softly against the pavement as she fell in step with him, her stride unwavering. There was no way she was letting this monster steal the new job she'd made here. She wouldn't let him force her to move jobs or move away out of fear.

Klein pushed up from her car, a smug look on his face as he eyed her. For a brief moment, when he glanced at Gerard, Zoe could see his mask slip a fraction. His expression was one of barely concealed rage, as if the monster inside him was clawing to get free, but just as quickly, it was gone, replaced by a charming-looking middle-aged man.

"You're on private property. Leave before I call the police," Gerard said, his voice clipped.

Damn, he got right to the point. Right now Zoe was grateful she'd bared her soul to the man.

Klein's eyes narrowed a fraction, but he didn't move any closer to them. Zoe remained where she was, about fifteen feet away from him, her legs simply refusing to work any longer. It didn't matter how angry she was, or how many times she'd played out this scenario in her mind, she was fucking terrified of this man. It was the deadness in his eyes. Now that she looked at him, truly looked, there was nothing inside his soul.

That was scary.

"Are you fucking her too?" Klein asked abruptly, his gaze narrowing on Gerard.

Damn it, no. She didn't want this psycho's attention on her friend and boss. Anger detonated inside her, shoving her fear out of the way. "Well, 'too' would imply that I've fucked you and we both know I haven't. And never will."

Aaaand, that did it. Klein's attention was back on her, that laser-like intensity unnerving. But she stood her ground. She refused to cower in front of him, not when she knew he craved it. He took a menacing step in their direction. Zoe tensed, her grip on her pepper spray tightening.

DEADLY FALLOUT | 23

Gerard jerked a thumb behind him. "Our security cameras send an automatic dump to an external server every few minutes. So you being here has been recorded. Even if you decide to be stupid and try to attack us then break in and erase the history, you'll never be able to cover anything up. So why don't you get the hell out of here and never come back? Because if I see you again, you won't get a warning." There was something deadly and serious about Gerard's voice. A tone Zoe had never heard before.

Klein's entire body drew taut as he went impossibly still, his dark eyes intent on her until just as suddenly, he relaxed and let out an eerie laugh. "Just wanted to stop by and see you, Zoe. Now that I'm back in town, I'm sure we'll be seeing more of each other." Turning away from them, he headed across the parking lot, his gait steady and unhurried.

Just like when she'd seen him leaving that hospital room months ago.

A shiver snaked down her spine. She kept her gaze on Klein until he got into a dark luxury sedan and steered out of the parking lot. As he sped away, she released a pent up sigh of relief and turned to Gerard. "That was an impressive threat." He was always so mild mannered and easy going. She felt as if she was seeing a different side of him.

"I don't like bullies." Jaw clenched tight, he finally looked back at Zoe when Klein's car pulled out of sight down the road.

"I'm filing a restraining order tonight," she said before he could continue. She'd filed a temporary one right before Klein had left, but it had expired a month ago. With him out of the country, she hadn't attempted to get it extended, mainly because she'd moved and she didn't want to list her new home address on it. Not when she'd gone to great lengths to hide where she was now living.

He nodded. "Good. I'm going with you."

Her first instinct was to argue that it wasn't necessary, but she knew that look of determination by now and the truth was, she didn't want to go alone. Instead of arguing she nodded. "If you're sure it won't affect you getting home in time for dinner?" Because she knew he loved having family dinners with his two teenage daughters every night. Especially since his wife had died a couple years ago.

Half-smiling, he shook his head. "My sister is with the girls. They're fine."

Palming her keys, she nodded, already feeling stronger. "Let's do this then."

* * *

DEADLY FALLOUT | 25

Zoe stood in front of the security desk at her friends Mina and Blue's high rise luxury condo. After filing a restraining order against Klein, she'd been too wired to go home. Well, and scared. Terrified that Klein had found a way to follow her, she'd checked her car for freaking trackers. She'd felt stupid doing it, but was relieved once she'd finished her inspection and found nothing.

After leaving the police station she'd driven around aimlessly for what felt like forever until finally she'd decided to come here. Their building had the best security she'd ever seen. The couple could certainly afford it and Blue was security-minded by nature, especially since his new wife had just inherited her father's billion-dollar empire, and he worked for Red Stone Security.

The twenty-something aged man behind the desk smiled politely at her as he placed the phone back in its cradle. Zoe was on their approved list of guests, but it was still late, and security didn't let anyone up without verbal approval. Not workers, friends, family, no one.

"You're cleared to go up, Ms. Hansen," he said, nodding toward the elevators where another two security guards stood like Roman sentries.

And these weren't typical security guys, not like the type they'd had at the hospital. Every single man or woman she'd seen here had a distinct military bearing and they were all visibly armed. Probably had hidden weapons too. Strangely, the sight of those guns actually made her feel safe.

A couple minutes later she stepped out into the lobby of the penthouse floor and found two more armed guards. She didn't recognize them, but knew they must work for Red Stone Security, the same company Blue and her brother worked for.

They nodded at her in that same polite way as the guard downstairs. Completely professional, but it was clear they were looking at her as if she might be packing heat or something. Before she'd taken two steps, the front door of the condo flew open.

Both men turned and went to stand in front of Mina protectively but she brushed past them, her arms outstretched. "Zoe! This is such a pleasant surprise."

And the woman meant it. The welcoming note in her voice did something to Zoe. She hadn't cried over the entire mess with Klein, not after her attack and not after the hospital treated her like garbage, forcing her to leave a job she loved. But seeing Mina opening her arms to her, Zoe lost it.

She burst into tears, clearly taking Mina off guard. Well, she'd taken herself off guard too. God, she hated crying—because it was embarrassing and she was an ugly crier. Ugh.

Zoe was vaguely aware of Mina wrapping her in a hug and ushering her into the plush place as tears blurred her vision. She should probably be more embarrassed but Mina was her friend and she knew she could be real with her.

"He's back," Zoe blurted as Mina led her to one of the couches in a spacious living room that overlooked downtown Miami. The city lights below were a kaleidoscope of bright colors, all blurred by the tears in her eyes. "I parked across the street but was careful not to be followed," she added, wiping the wetness on her cheeks away as she managed to get herself under control.

Mina just snorted softly. "This place is a fortress, don't worry about that. So . . . you're sure he's back?" she asked as she sat next to her, turning her body to face Zoe's.

She nodded. "Oh yeah, he showed up at my work." Just thinking about that made her shiver.

When Mina let out a surprising curse, Zoe smiled, the small action loosening something inside her chest.

Her friend stood and moved to the small mini-bar by the window, grabbing two glasses and a bottle of red wine before sitting back down next to her. "Tell me everything."

Twenty minutes later Zoe had unloaded everything that had happened, including her trip to the police station and that she'd finally told her brother about what was going on. He was in California on a job now so she felt even worse that she'd unloaded so much with him out of town. He'd been pissed that she'd withheld something so important, and in typical Vincent fashion, he'd threatened to kill Klein. She wouldn't admit it to anyone, but that was the real reason she hadn't told her brother before.

As a former SEAL, Vincent wouldn't have a problem defending her against a psycho. But she didn't want him to do something he couldn't take back, something that could affect his career and the rest of his life. He'd worked so hard to get to where he was and she couldn't ever be responsible for him ending up in jail.

Mina leaned back against the couch, wine glass in hand, her finger idly tracing down the stem. Zoe noticed that Mina hadn't actually drank anything, but didn't comment as her friend set the glass down on the table next to her. "So the restraining order bars him from coming to your work?"

Zoe nodded. "Yes. And I'll be making copies of it for everyone at work and including his photo so they know who he is." She just hadn't listed her home address on the order. Considering Klein knew where she worked, which wasn't a surprise since people she used to work with were aware of her new job, she hadn't wanted to make it easy for him to find her house in case he didn't know yet. Because a piece of paper wouldn't stop him from coming after her. It would certainly get him in trouble with the law if he broke the order, but if he decided to attack her, she'd still be injured or dead, piece of paper or not.

After his attack at the hospital, he'd been smart about harassing her, making sure nothing could be traced back to him, but she knew he'd slashed her tires, stolen her mail, and sent her too many anonymous, vile texts from a burner phone to count until finally she'd changed her phone number. The police had actually believed her. But believing her was one thing. The State's Attorney wouldn't press charges against someone like Braddock Klein—upstanding citizen with a lot of politically powerful friends—without hard evidence. The justice system was so broken it made her want to cry. Or punch something.

Mina started to say something when a soft chime filled the room, the alert letting them know someone had entered the front door.

"Mina? Is Zoe here?" Blue called out from the front of the condo as Mina stood.

Zoe followed suit and realized she still had her jacket on—and still felt cold despite the warmth in the room. It was a bone-deep kind of chill, one that had nothing to do with the temperature.

A second later Blue and another man entered the living room, both dressed in suits. It took Zoe a moment to recognize the guy. Dark hair, piercing green eyes, about six feet of raw muscle that a suit couldn't hide. Sawyer

McCabe. Navy SEAL, or maybe former, if he was working with Blue now. The last time she'd seen him, he'd
punched her brother in the face.

Zoe withheld a groan. Just freaking great. She had
enough to deal with without some jackass who'd tried to
hurt her little brother being present to hear all her drama.

CHAPTER TWO

Braddock Klein wrapped his fingers around the glass tumbler, trying to temper the rage burning inside him as he stared out at the Atlantic Ocean. The spectacular view from his lanai normally soothed him, but nothing could do that now. He couldn't believe the way Zoe had spoken to him after all the time they'd been apart, and in front of someone else no less.

Dr. Gerard Fernandez was a prick. Braddock had met him at different functions over the last decade and couldn't stand the guy. So self-righteous about everything. It wasn't like Fernandez did any pro bono or charity work, not like Braddock did. Something Zoe should be able to clearly see. Why couldn't she see how good they'd be together? How right they were for each other?

After spending six months in South America working for Medicine Without Borders, he'd come back ready to start something with Zoe. He knew she was angry at him for what had happened at the hospital, but she shouldn't have played so hard to get with him. She should *know* that she belonged to him. He'd made his intentions clear long ago and she'd seemed receptive, always so friendly at work. Until that night when she'd completely overreacted to his advances.

He'd even left his wife for her. Right before he'd gone to South America he'd started the divorce proceedings. His lawyer was brilliant and everything had gone smoothly. He was paying out the ass for the divorce but it was worth it. Especially since he knew he could be paying a lot more.

For some reason his ex-wife hadn't fought him at all. She'd just taken what was owed her in their prenuptial agreement and walked away without a fight. She'd tried to leave him once two years ago but he'd made it clear that no one walked away from him. Ever since then she'd done nothing but try to please him. It had been so tiring. Being rid of her was one of the best things that could have happened to him.

Now he could focus all his attention on Zoe. Like she deserved. She was a smart, talented woman and deserved to be with someone like him. She was knowledgeable about their industry, could hold intelligent conversations with their peers, and was an incredibly calm surgeon. She'd never gotten rattled during surgeries, had always been cool and focused. That alone was a turn-on. Plus she was beautiful so he could take her anywhere. That nonsense from the hospital would blow over eventually. It was just a misunderstanding and he would forgive her for embarrassing him. Of course he'd

DEADLY FALLOUT | 33

have to punish her, but he wouldn't hold it over her head forever.

When he realized his tumbler was empty he started to stand—only to discover he wasn't alone. As he faced the glass doors that led to his living room, he frowned at the tall, lithe woman standing there with her hands on her hips.

"What are you doing here?" His gaze went to the Scotch bottle in her hand and his frown deepened. He hated it when she made herself feel at home. He'd barely been back in the country and here she was. Annoying him.

With a tinkling laugh, she glided toward him, her hips swaying seductively. Despite the cooler temperature and the breeze coming up off the ocean, she wore a skin tight neon purple dress that accentuated all her curves. The puffy jacket she wore looked as if it was for fashion, not warmth. She had a tight body, one she worked hard to keep, but strip it away and there wasn't much underneath. She'd been a good fuck, nothing more. It was deeply disturbing the way she kept trying to insert herself back into his life. All those emails and phone calls while he'd been away. He knew she wasn't that bright, which was one of the reasons he'd originally hooked up with her, but she was clearly persistent.

"I heard you were back in town and couldn't believe you hadn't called." Her lips pulled down into a faux pouty frown and he noticed she wasn't wearing her normal bright red lipstick.

How the hell had she known . . . Damn it, fucking social media. He'd gotten an alert that the hospital had posted something about his return. He'd wanted to fly under the radar for a couple weeks, but he should have expected that someone as important as him wouldn't go unnoticed for long. Well, if she was here, maybe he could get something out of her visit. He tilted his head at the bottle in her hand before he sat back in his chair. "Is that for me?"

Sighing, she moved toward him, her heels clicking on the tile as she opened the bottle. She poured him a glass before spreading her legs and straddling him. Her puffy, feathery jacket brushed against his face as she sat on him. "You're in a mood. Did the South America trip not go well?"

His gaze dipped to her mouth as she spoke and he started to get hard. The woman could give some serious head. He wondered if she'd blow him then leave. No, that would be too much wishful thinking. She'd want to stay and talk afterward. "It was fine. I'm just tired after traveling."

She shifted slightly over him, her dress riding up on her thighs as she rubbed herself over his growing dick. "Is that for me?" she murmured, leaning down to nip his ear between her teeth.

He slid his hands around her, letting them settle on her hips. Pushing out a sigh, he leaned his head back. "I'm not really in the mood." He knew if he said that, she'd give him what he wanted and he wouldn't have to do any work. And after he got what he wanted, he'd make up an excuse about having to get up early tomorrow and kick her out.

She leaned back then, her dark eyes flashing with anger. One of her hands tightened on his shoulder and the other slid around to the back of his neck. She usually liked it rough, maybe he'd make time for her tonight after all.

"Not in the mood? Could've fooled me," she snapped.

Damn, time to placate her. "It's not that. I . . . my divorce is just final and I've been in a shithole for the last six months. I'm exhausted and you know what I need." He dropped his voice, sounding apologetic.

Her lips pursed. "If you're so exhausted how did you have the time to go see Zoe Hansen tonight?"

He jerked in his seat, sitting up straighter. Alarm surged through him. He hadn't told anyone he'd gone to see Zoe. "How the hell did you—"

A sudden, sharp pain pierced his neck as she sliced across his jugular. He lurched forward, his hands on her hips tightening as blood sprayed everywhere, covering her face and clothes. *Blood?*

That was when he saw the flash of metal in her hand as she slid off him. Crimson stained her stupid jacket as she laughed crazily, a knife gripped tightly in her fingers. He slapped a hand to his neck, trying to stop the gushing. He stood, his legs wobbling, but he forced himself to remain upright.

She took a step back, watching him gleefully, her eyes completely crazy.

His knees shook, but he had to stand, to get help. Sitting would accelerate the blood loss. Help. He had to call for help. He fumbled in his pants pocket and grabbed his phone. It slipped from his fingers because of all the blood. As it landed on the tile, she laughed again.

"That's what you get, stupid fuck," she spat, turning on her heel and stomping toward the open sliding glass door.

He took a step after her, but fell to his knees, the impact jarring him, but he barely felt the pain. The blood was spurting out, not leaking so the bitch must have cut an artery. He opened his mouth, trying to speak, but a rush of pain overwhelmed him as blood gurgled up from the wound. He tried to hold his wound but his hands were too slick and his vision was turning dark.

No! This stupid bitch couldn't have killed him. He refused to die like this. No, no...

* * *

Sawyer tried not to stare at Zoe as she smoothed a hand down the front of her wool coat and made her way around the couch to hug Alex. Or Blue, as almost everyone else called him.

But hell, it was hard not to watch her. Petite and compact with smooth mocha skin and intelligent dark eyes, nothing got past that woman. He vividly remembered the last time he'd seen her and inwardly cringed. He didn't regret punching her brother, but he did regret doing it in front of an audience. Especially since she'd been there.

He'd only met her a couple times before that encounter and each time he'd been too damn nervous to talk to her. Big, bad SEAL couldn't talk to a small woman with luscious curves and a smart mouth he'd had way too many fantasies about. Her hair was shorter now, the corkscrew curls bouncing everywhere. Years ago she'd worn it long and straight. He liked this version of her too.

He jerked out of his haze when he realized Blue was talking to him. "Sawyer, this is Zoe Hansen, Vincent's sister."

Sawyer started to say they'd already met before when Zoe held out a hand, her expression polite. "Nice to meet you."

What the fuck? She didn't remember him? That shouldn't annoy him as much as it did. Talk about a blow to his ego. He gritted his teeth and tried to force a polite smile as he returned her handshake. God, her hands were soft too. That was when he realized how red her eyes were, as if she'd been crying. He frowned. "You okay?"

Just like that her polite expression went completely blank. "I'm good, thank you." Then she cleared her throat and looked pointedly at Blue.

His friend gave a short nod before looking back at Mina and Sawyer. "We're going to be in my office for a few minutes but make yourself at home."

"Come on, I'll get you something to drink," Mina said, smiling and motioning to the mini-bar. "How's this week gone?"

Tearing his attention from Zoe's retreating backside, he turned to Mina and smiled as she poured him a bourbon. "Good. Learned a lot."

Laughing lightly, she shook her head and handed him the drink before dropping onto one of the couches. "Such a succinct answer. You're as bad as Alex."

"You really want to hear about the protocol review and training exercises we did?" After a twenty-year Navy career, he'd recently retired at thirty-seven and had taken a job with Red Stone Security heading up one of their

DEADLY FALLOUT | 39

East Coast divisions. And this was his last week of training under Alex.

It was still too soon to decide, but Sawyer was going with his gut that this was the best damn move he could have ever made career-wise. He'd been offered jobs by multiple government agencies, but the political bullshit he'd have had to deal with had held him back from accepting. When Porter Caldwell, one of the owners of Red Stone had contacted him, he'd internally jumped at the offer. He'd made Porter wait for his answer because he'd wanted to negotiate his hiring terms, but taking this job had been a no-brainer.

Mina pursed her lips together. "Well, I don't need *all* the details." She started to say something else when a soft bell dinged.

He knew from being invited over here on multiple occasions that was the timer for the oven. They had a chef who came by four or five days a week and prepared dinner for them. Since he hadn't seen or heard their chef, he assumed she'd gone home for the evening. Sawyer automatically stood. "I'll get it . . . What did Marcelle make tonight?"

Smiling, Mina stood. "Herb-roasted lamb with a side of potatoes, butternut squash soup and a spinach salad. And you don't have to get anything."

He just grunted. "You shouldn't be doing anything anyway." A week ago Alex and Mina had told Sawyer that Mina was fourteen weeks pregnant. He didn't know anything about pregnant women but she probably shouldn't be lifting stuff.

"Seriously, don't even start with me," she muttered, nudging him out of the way with her hip. "I only get nauseous in the mornings and I think I can handle pulling a glass pan out of the oven."

Ignoring her, Sawyer headed into the kitchen and took the oven mitts left on the counter before opening up one of the ovens. Their kitchen was one of those state-of-the-art types with commercial grade appliances that probably rivaled the best restaurants in the city. Especially the stainless steel double oven with a sixty inch range and a built-in broiler with a raised griddle. He'd learned to cook at a young age—thanks to his mom, he and all his brothers had—and found it was something he enjoyed immensely. Good thing too, since he'd been single most of his life. He'd love a spread like this.

"You always look at that oven like you want to marry it," Mina said lightly.

Snorting, he pulled out the giant pan and set it on the stove top before turning it off. "I don't know if I'd go that far," he said, lifting the lid to the soup. The rich scent was perfect. "I can leave this simmering or turn it off, depending on how long Zoe and Alex will be?" He phrased it as a question because, yeah, he was digging for information. He hadn't liked the sight of Zoe crying at all and he wanted to know what was going on. And he wasn't above fishing.

Crossing her arms around her middle, Mina leaned against one of the counters next to a covered tray of assorted cheeses Marcelle must have left out. "I don't know how long they're going to be."

"Something going on with your friend?" Screw the subtle art of fishing.

Mina bit her bottom lip. She glanced at the entryway, then back at Sawyer, her dark green eyes filled with worry. "Yes. I don't think it's a secret either." She fidgeted with the hem of her sweater before sighing and continuing. "She has a stalker. The guy's been out of the country for the last six months but he's back a week early and stopped by her work tonight to harass her. It really rattled her."

That hadn't been what he'd been expecting at all. "She has a stalker and Vincent hasn't . . . taken care of the problem?" At one time Sawyer and Vincent had had some issues but no matter what Sawyer thought of him, Vincent was the type of guy to take care of his family, by legal means or otherwise. No way he'd let some asshole harass his sister without doing something about it.

"She only recently told Vincent. As in, earlier tonight." Sighing, Mina headed for the stainless steel refrigerator and pulled out a bottle of sparkling water. "Alex has been monitoring the guy as best he could, but obviously he got back into the country without him knowing. I'm sure he's trying to figure out what happened as we speak."

"What's the stalker's name?" Sawyer asked before he could stop himself. This wasn't his deal, had nothing to do with him, but . . . fuck. If Zoe had a stalker and hadn't even told her brother about it until today, someone needed to look into this guy further. It might as well be him.

Mina paused and for a long moment he thought she wasn't going to tell him. Finally she sighed and sat down at the center island, exhaustion he was pretty sure was from her pregnancy, on her face. "Braddock Klein."

Braddock Klein. Sawyer filed that name away and vowed to put a stop to Zoe's stalker situation.

CHAPTER THREE

Zoe stepped into Blue's office. Instead of the giant, masculine furniture she'd expected it was all wood, glass and sleek looking décor. And of course paintings by Mina graced two of the walls. The third 'wall' was all windows, overlooking the city, and the last was lined with built-in bookshelves.

"So, how far along is Mina?"

Blue shot her a surprised glance over his shoulder as he made his way to his glass-topped desk. He picked up a remote control and pressed a couple buttons. A soft humming sound filled the room as blinds descended from the top of the windows, covering the floor-to-ceiling length expanse. "How'd you know?"

Zoe shrugged, glad she'd guessed right. They'd make great parents. "She didn't drink her wine tonight and I've been around enough pregnant women to know one when I see one. She kept holding her stomach almost protectively."

Blue's face split into a wide, unexpected grin. Zoe had known him for a long time thanks to his friendship with Vincent and the man was always so damn serious. Until Mina. She'd definitely been the best thing to ever happen to her friend. "It's unexpected and we haven't told many people, but fourteen weeks."

"How's she doing? Any morning sickness?" It was an outdated term since pregnancy related nausea could happen at any time of the day.

"She's good but gets a little nauseated in the mornings. Her doctor said that's normal though?" He phrased the last part as a question, a thread of panic invading his voice.

Smiling, she nodded. "Totally normal. Who's her OB?"

When Blue named the best obstetrics doctor in not only the city, but probably the East Coast, she nodded her approval. "Good."

Blue motioned toward a sleek, but comfortable-looking leather couch near the now covered window. It was angled in between the window and one of the bookshelves and had a throw blanket and Mina's ereader on it. Zoe guessed her friend relaxed in here while Blue worked sometimes. The thought made her smile, despite the turmoil surging through her. He slid the stuff to the side as they sat.

"Tell me what happened," Blue said quietly, all business.

Zoe launched into another recap of the evening, feeling stronger the second time she recounted what had

DEADLY FALLOUT | 45

happened. When she was done, Blue's jaw tightened as he stood and snagged his laptop from his desk.

Wordlessly he turned it on and clicked away until finally he stopped, frowning. He shook his head then shot her a concerned look. "I've had Lizzy tracking Klein—I didn't tell her the reason—and I've received no alerts that he's used his credit card or other accounts at any foreign airports or back here in Miami. The use of any of his accounts would have alerted us he was on the move. Not even his cell phone pinged . . ." Sighing, he cursed under his breath. "Never mind. Lizzy's system just sent an alert that his phone reactivated in Miami an hour ago."

Zoe didn't care how he'd returned undetected, she just cared that he was here and a big problem. "He could have paid all in cash and he probably flew in on a medical flight. I'm pretty sure he came straight from the airport to see me. God, it was so creepy seeing him again. I was just starting to feel normal." And she wasn't going to let that psycho take that away from her.

"We're going to stop this guy." His voice was serious, making her feel a little better.

"I've got a good alarm system and I took your advice. I've been going to the gun range every week without fail."

"If he violates his restraining order the police will actually have something against him, but . . . he has no

priors and he's got a lot of powerful friends." Blue's expression was grim.

Zoe knew how broken the system was, especially after working in the ER for so many years. It was how
she'd developed friendships with a lot of Miami PD officers. It would have been impossible not to with her
job. She knew more than most how things worked. If
Klein violated the restraining order, he'd get in trouble,
but he wouldn't end up doing any jail time. Not with his
lawyers. Not unless he actually hurt her. And he was too
smart to overtly violate it. Last time he'd sent so many
disgusting texts, but they'd all been from burner phones
and there had been no way to track them back to Klein
as the purchaser.

She wrapped her arms around herself, fighting off a
chill. After six months of peace she'd almost forgotten
how tense and stressed she'd become before Klein had
left the country. Now the ugliness was all rushing back.

"I'd like it if you'd sleep here tonight. We've got a big
guest room and—"

"Okay."

Blue blinked in surprise. "Thought I'd have to con-
vince you more."

"Seriously?"

He lifted one big shoulder. "You can be stubborn
sometimes."

DEADLY FALLOUT | 47

She knew he was referring to her not telling Vincent, but that wasn't really stubbornness so much as watching out for her brother. But okay, she *could* be stubborn. "Not about my safety. If that psycho came to see me immediately after getting back into town, I'm not risking anything. And thank you, I really appreciate the offer. I'll have to go home in the morning before work, but the thought of going there right now alone is a little terrifying." She hated Klein for making her so scared. Soon she wanted to take all that power back from him. She just needed to figure out how.

"I'm going to have one of my guys follow you home tomorrow and make sure you get to work safely. I'd do it myself but I've got a big meeting in the morning. A potential new Red Stone client." His expression was apologetic.

"I should probably say you don't have to do that but . . . I'm taking you up on your offer." Because she wasn't gambling with her life. "Thank you, again. I—"

He shook his head. "I don't want your thanks. I just want you safe."

"I know." Her eyes started to well up again, but she quickly blinked away the tears.

Blue stared at her like a deer caught in headlights. Probably because he'd never seen her cry. She normally took everything in stride, had been doing it since she was a kid. Her dad had been like that and she was glad she'd gotten that personality trait. It was one of the things that made her a good doctor. She cared for her patients but she was able to compartmentalize her emotions. Until now.

Now she was like a leaky faucet and she didn't like it. Soon enough she was going to take back the power from that psycho Klein. She just had to figure out how.

* * *

Zoe finished zipping up her black slacks and smoothed a hand down the front of her sweater. Mina had given her something to sleep in last night, but she was wearing the same clothes she'd left work in yesterday. Not that she cared. After a steaming hot shower this morning and a peaceful night's sleep, she felt more focused about everything.

And her hair looked amazing, which she knew was a stupidly small thing in all this, but for some reason, it gave her confidence a huge boost. She had a lot of hair, but it was incredibly fine. Luckily Mina had pretty much every beauty product imaginable, including what Zoe needed to tame her mass of curls. When Zoe had been younger she'd hated her curly hair. It had taken a lot of trial and error to figure out what worked for her, but now she loved it.

Today, it was part of her armor as she faced the world again. The world which her crazy stalker had waltzed back into.

Shaking her head at herself, she picked up her coat from the bed and headed out. Her feet were silent against the hardwood floors as she made her way down the hallway to the kitchen. She was surprised to hear a male voice since she knew that Blue had said he was leaving early this morning, but then remembered their security. For the most part Mina's daily security wasn't inside her condo with her until she started working in her art studio. Then they took up residence in the condo. But Mina was so sweet she probably invited them in for coffee every morning.

As Zoe entered the kitchen, all the breath left her lungs in a whoosh. *Sawyer McCabe.* Damn that sexy man, what was he doing here?

"Zoe," Mina said, smiling warmly at her. "How'd you sleep?"

She stepped farther into the room, a smile pulling at her lips. "Surprisingly good. I was going to strip the sheets, but then just made the bed since I wasn't sure what you wanted me to do, and..." She shrugged nervously. *Oh my God, stop rambling*, she ordered her frazzled brain. She always did that when she was feeling out of sorts and being around Sawyer put her on edge. She wasn't exactly sure why, but it probably had to do with

the way her body heated up just being around him—
even though he'd once punched her brother in the face.
The reaction was so visceral and so unlike her and she
didn't like wanting someone whom her brother didn't
like. She was thankful her bra covered her hardening
nipples.

"It's fine. You remember Sawyer from last night."
Mina nodded at Sawyer, who was intently watching Zoe
now.

Forcing her mouth to work, she found a polite smile
and nodded. "Yes, nice to see you again."

Instead of a suit, today he wore dark gray pants and a
black sweater that couldn't hide his strong physique.
Even though he leaned casually against one of the counters in Mina's gorgeous kitchen, holding a cup of coffee,
he looked anything but relaxed. His body was pulled
taut, alert, as if he was ready for danger at any moment.
Her brother was the same way. Definitely a SEAL thing,
though she'd learned from Blue last night that Sawyer
wasn't in the Navy anymore, but now worked for Red
Stone Security in a management position. She knew it
was pretty rare for someone to be hired on directly to
management with them so this guy had to have a seriously impressive résumé.

"You too. There's coffee if you want to grab some before you leave or we can stop somewhere." That warm,

honeyed voice rolled over her, making her fight off a shiver.

Until it registered what he'd said. Frowning, she looked between him and Mina, then back to him. "You're coming with me?" she asked.

Nodding, he headed toward the sink where he started rinsing out his mug. "I thought Blue told you that you'd have an escort today."

"He did, but..." She cleared her throat, not sure how to continue. Blue had told her that he was sending one of his guys with her to her house, but she'd assumed it would be one of his normal guys who stayed with Mina.

"Oh, Sawyer is highly trained. He was a SEAL, just like Vincent," Mina said, clearly misinterpreting Zoe's hesitation.

"Thank you," she said, because really, that was all she could come up with at the moment. There was no way she could explain her hesitation. "And I don't need coffee. I'll just grab some at work." Right about now she was really thankful it was Friday and that she wasn't one of the on-call doctors this weekend.

Sawyer turned from the sink and looked at her with an unreadable expression and nodded. "Do you need to get anything else?"

She shook her head before focusing on Mina. After hugging her and saying goodbye, she found herself alone in the custom-made, wood-lined elevator with Sawyer.

"Thank you for coming with me." Normally she didn't need to fill silences, but she desperately felt the urge right now.

He nodded once, his posture alert and perfect as he stared ahead at the closed doors. "You're welcome. We've met before, by the way." His voice was tight, controlled.

"I know," she blurted before she could stop herself.

He glanced down at her, real surprise in his green eyes. "You remembered?"

She nodded and felt a blush heating up her cheeks. "I was embarrassed yesterday and just . . . reacted poorly I think. I didn't want anyone else to see me like that. Blue and Mina are fine, but you're virtually a stranger and I just . . . I'm sorry." Because what else was there to say?

His expression softened and he turned toward the doors as they opened up. "Well, I'm sorry the last time we saw each other that I punched your brother."

Despite the tenseness humming through her, she snorted and stepped out into the lobby with him. "Somehow I doubt you're actually sorry about punching Vincent." While she wasn't sure what had gone down between the two of them, Sawyer didn't seem like the type of man to regret things or to attack someone lightly.

"I'm sorry I did it in front of you," he amended, not looking at her as he scanned the lobby and sitting area.

Bright sunlight streamed in through the glass windows and doors, illuminating the crystal and chrome chandeliers overhead, making the entire space sparkle beautifully.

His response lightened her mood even more. Not completely, because nothing could do that. Not when she was in the position that she needed an escort simply to go home and to work. She did feel incredibly safe with Sawyer though.

Vincent was still out of town but was going to try to come home early. Even though she didn't want to affect her brother's job, she was truly glad he'd be returning to Miami soon. He might be the baby of the family but he'd always been a rock for her and her sisters after their father had died.

"I would deny this under torture because I love my brother, but . . . I'm betting it wasn't completely unprovoked."

Sawyer looked down at her as they reached one set of glass doors, his eyebrows drawing together. "He didn't tell you what it was about?"

She shook her head. Vincent had seemed almost embarrassed by it and she hadn't wanted to push. Not when he'd been dealing with so much back then.

Sawyer didn't respond, just opened the door. Instead of letting her go first, like she'd expected, he moved outside in front of her, using his body as a barrier as he scanned the relatively quiet street. Two women jogged by on the sidewalk, both with earbuds in as they pounded the pavement. Then an older, white-haired man walking a small dog with white-and-black fur strolled by carrying a Starbucks cup. Nothing seemed out of the ordinary.

Sawyer must have agreed, because he gave an almost imperceptible nod before looking back at her. "First we're going to get your car. I'm going to scan it for any tracking devices or . . . anything. Then you're going to drive me to my truck, which is just a block from here—I couldn't find a spot any closer. From there, I'm going to follow you home. Blue's filled me in on what's going on so I'd like to shadow you at your work today, see if that fucker shows up. He's going to be notified of the restraining order, probably already has been so if he's pissed enough, he'll show up at your work. If we can document that, it's a start."

His words made her chest tighten as she realized she had no choice but to face her new reality head on. She wouldn't have an escort every day, but for now, she was glad to have someone on her side—someone trained—who had an idea how to tackle today. She still needed to make copies of her restraining order and give them out to everyone at work, but today suddenly seemed manageable with Sawyer by her side.

"Thank you for doing this."

"I don't need your thanks," he said brusquely before turning toward the road and glancing both ways.

Oh right, this was just a job for him. Well, job or not, she was still damn thankful for his presence.

CHAPTER FOUR

Sawyer parked his truck behind Zoe's two-door car, automatically scanning the exterior of her house and neighbors' homes. It was eight a.m. so some people were already leaving; parents with kids and others dressed in business attire. No one appeared out of the ordinary and no one looked like Braddock Klein.

Blue had sent him a detailed file on Klein last night after Sawyer had more or less volunteered to shadow Zoe today. His friend had planned to use one of Mina's security guys to trail Zoe, but Sawyer was having none of that. His training was officially over today and he started with his new team on Monday. They could put someone else on her then if necessary. But he wanted to look out for her now and over the weekend, and he wasn't going to examine why too closely. He just knew he wanted her safe. He also knew that had nothing to do with a sense of duty because she was Vincent's sister and everything to do with her specifically. The woman intrigued him.

Shutting his door behind him, he met Zoe as she was getting out of her car. A breeze blew up and her curls bounced softly in the wind. An unbidden image of what it would feel like to run his fingers through her hair while she was naked and under him entered his mind, but he locked that down. He was on the job and her safety was more important than his fucking libido.

"Did it seem as if anyone was following us?" she asked, an anxious frown creasing her brow.

"Nope." He was good at locating a single tail, but if someone was working with a full team or in tandem with a partner, then it became more difficult. Since Klein seemed to be a one-man stalker, Sawyer was almost certain they hadn't been followed.

"Thank God," she muttered, glancing around nervously.

Yeah, what Sawyer wouldn't give to kick this guy's ass. Seeing fear on Zoe's face sliced at him. He'd spent most of his adult life fighting terrorists and when you got right down to it, they were nothing but psychotic bullies who wanted the world to see everything their way. Now everything about Zoe's life was being affected by a bully with an ego. That brought out all his protective instincts whether he wanted it to or not. "You set your alarm yesterday, right?"

She nodded and palmed her keys. "Yes, so if it's off..." She trailed off, not needing to finish.

After they entered her house, the insistent beep of her alarm sounded and he could see the tension leave her body as she pressed the code into the keypad. He locked the front door behind them then ordered her to stay put. Her eyes widened at his tone, but he didn't have time to reassure her. He needed to sweep her house.

Withdrawing his SIG, he held it at his side as he methodically swept each room. She had a three-bedroom, two-bath home in a higher end part of town and close to the practice she worked at. Her neighborhood had lake access, though her house wasn't on the water and from the file Blue had given him, they had twenty-four-seven security driving around or sitting in the guard house he'd seen when they'd entered the subdivision. But it didn't appear to be actually gated, something he hadn't liked. He planned to ask her about that later.

Once he was certain the house was secure he found Zoe standing in her foyer next to an oversized floor vase, her arms crossed over her chest. "House is secure."

"Thank you. And next time, if there is one, *ask* me to stay put, don't order me around."

He'd taken plenty of orders in the Navy, but for the most part he'd given them, especially on missions. His instinct was to tell her that he'd just been doing his job, but he could stand to use some finesse, especially where Zoe was concerned. "My apologies."

She blinked, her arms dropping. "Really?"

He lifted an eyebrow. "You want me to argue?"

"No, I . . . it's nice to be talking to a grownup, that's all." She gave him a real smile then, a megawatt one that lit up her face and it was all for him. The sight was a kick to his chest, stealing all the breath from his lungs. "I already showered so I just need to change then snag a cup of coffee. I have one of those one-cup machines so if you want, feel free to brew yourself a cup. Or we can just grab some at my work."

He nodded and started to respond when a sharp knock on her front door had him straightening. He turned, blocking her body with his as he reached for his weapon.

"Miami PD, open the door," a loud male voice said.

Sawyer's first instinct was that this was a trap. He moved to the peephole and peered through, aware of Zoe right behind him. There were three men, two wearing police uniforms and one man wearing a suit and tie. Two cruisers were parked at the curb out front. "Show some ID," he demanded. Sawyer had no clue how devious Klein was and he wasn't taking any chances with Zoe's safety.

The man in the suit straightened and faced the peephole directly. "Zoe, you in there? Answer me." His tone was concerned.

Zoe's hand on Sawyer's forearm made him look down. "It's okay, that's Carlito Duarte. He's a detective with the police department." She turned from him and unlocked the door. When she opened it, Sawyer knew immediately that whatever was going on, was bad.

All three men looked grim, especially the detective. The man looked at Sawyer and assessed him before focusing on Zoe. "Zoe Hansen, I have a warrant for your arrest for the murder of Braddock Klein."

"What?" she gasped, reeling back a step.

Klein was dead? Well that solved one of her problems, but this was just fucked up. Sawyer wanted to haul her back from the men, but knew he'd just make the situation a hell of a lot worse if he got in the way. Because this had to be a setup, no doubt about it.

The detective with bronzed skin, gray eyes and a GQ thing going on, nodded. "You have the right to an attorney and I'm telling you to exercise that right and not say a fucking word. Got it?" he asked her, his expression tight. Sawyer could tell the man hated doing this part of his job with Zoe.

Zoe's expression was one of horror and shock. She looked up at Sawyer as if he could somehow fix the situation. And hell if he wasn't going to try.

"Don't say a word," he told her. "I'm calling Alex and your brother right now. Where are you taking her?" he asked, turning his attention to the detective.

"Down to the station."

Sawyer nodded and looked at Zoe again as one of the officers stepped forward with handcuffs in his hand. *Fuck, no.* He didn't want to let her go and it was clear the detective didn't like this any better than she did. The sight of the cuffs made Zoe jerk with shock, but she didn't try to resist.

"Tell my brother to call our family lawyer and my mom," she blurted. "And call Gerard Fernandez. He's my boss. Alex has his information. I don't know what's going on, but he was with me before I went to Blue's last night..." She trailed off as Duarte stilled the man in uniform with the restraints.

"We'll cuff her in the cruiser and her hands go in front," he said quietly.

Not much, but it was a small show of courtesy, telling Sawyer all he needed to know about the detective. "I'm following you right now and making those calls. You're not going to jail so just stay quiet until your lawyer gets there, okay? I'm not kidding. Not one *single* word."

Swallowing hard, she nodded, her big brown eyes wide with fear as she let the officers escort her to the waiting police cruiser. What the hell was happening? If Klein had been murdered that was damn fast police work for them to have a suspect already. And there was no way in hell they'd have shown up on Zoe's doorstep and actually *arrested* her without physical evidence. Sawyer had a decent understanding of civilian law, more so now because of his new job, and it was too soon for the police to be here without concrete proof. Something else

DEADLY FALLOUT | 63

was going on and Sawyer was damn sure going to find out what it was and make sure Zoe got out of this mess.

The only silver lining in all this was that her stalker was no longer a problem.

* * *

"She's going to be okay," Sawyer said to Tanice Hansen, Zoe's mom, who was pacing nervously at the far end of the rectangular, cheap wood table.

They'd been taken to a quiet conference room at the police station, courtesy of Detective Duarte, whom Sawyer had recently discovered was friends with a lot of guys from Red Stone Security and had interacted with Zoe frequently when she'd worked at the hospital. Mina and Blue were both in different rooms being questioned by detectives to corroborate Zoe's alibi. And Sawyer knew that Blue had already had the security feeds from his condo sent over to the police for analyzing.

"I just can't believe anyone would think she'd even be capable of taking a life. She took the Hippocratic Oath and that means something to my girl. And I still can't believe she didn't tell me about any of this." A pop of anger sounded in the petite woman's voice. She was the same height as Zoe with flawless, darker skin. She looked decades younger than Sawyer guessed she had to be. Right now worry was evident in every taut line of her body.

"It's normal in a situation like this to keep what happened private from those closest to her." And Sawyer had already been in contact with Vincent who was currently on his way back to Miami.

Tanice frowned and swiveled toward him, hands on her hips. "How is that normal to keep something so big from her mother?"

"I'm just guessing, but Zoe probably felt ashamed, possibly embarrassed. She probably tried to think of all the different ways she could have seen this sooner, maybe prevented it from happening." One of Sawyer's guys had been stalked years ago and had been in a state of denial that it was happening to him, especially since it was another male doing the stalking. He figured Zoe had probably been in denial for a while too, made easier since Klein had been out of the country. It was a normal, human reaction.

Tanice's eyebrows furrowed together. "That makes no sense, she couldn't have prevented some crazy from focusing on her."

"We know that and intellectually Zoe knows that. But self-blame is a common effect on stalking victims." He was just impressed how well Zoe had been holding up.

DEADLY FALLOUT | 65

Losing her steam, Tanice pulled out a chair and collapsed into it. "You'd think that once your kids were out of the house and had families and lives of their own you could stop worrying. But you never do." Her eyes started to well with tears, but she looked away from him, angrily swatting at the wetness. The action reminded him so much of Zoe.

Realizing she didn't want him to see her upset, he stood from his chair and headed for the door. "I'll grab us some more drinks." He'd had way too much coffee the past couple hours while they waited so he'd be grabbing water.

"Thank you."

The door opened before he'd reached it. Zoe, Blue, Mina and Duarte stepped in. Zoe's eyes were red-rimmed, but she also looked relieved. Okay, that was a good thing. As she rushed toward her mother who'd already jumped from her chair, Sawyer looked between Blue and the detective. Zoe's attorney wasn't with them, which surprised Sawyer. Maybe the guy was filling out paperwork or he wasn't needed anymore.

Duarte shut the door behind him so they all had privacy.

"She's free?" Sawyer asked, needing to hear the words.

Duarte and Blue nodded at the same time. "Yes, thanks to a rock solid alibi," Duarte said. "If she hadn't stayed with you guys last night..." The man shook his head, his mouth still pulled into that grim line.

Sawyer only knew the basics at this point. That Klein had been found dead at his home, his throat cut. Zoe's fingerprint had been on the knife, but nowhere else at the scene. "So what happened?" he asked, not bothering to wait until he was alone with Blue. He figured Zoe's mom needed details now too.

"Someone called in an anonymous tip that Klein had been murdered late last night. They gave a description of a woman leaving his place who looked a lot like Zoe. Since she'd just filed a restraining order against him last night . . . well, Klein had powerful friends so there's a push to get this solved. Since she was a viable suspect, the techs ran her prints from the hospital against the single print on the knife and it's a match. Luckily there's no DNA of hers at the scene and her alibi is airtight. And the single print is . . . interesting."

Sawyer didn't respond, but he understood the man's meaning. One single print and no DNA at a crime scene? Unlikely. Someone planted that print.

"The time stamps on the security of her arriving at Alex and Mina's and witness statements from both of them are hugely helpful. The State's Attorney won't be pursuing criminal charges and we're now hunting for the real killer."

Sawyer had a lot of questions, like had they started looking for who'd called in that anonymous tip, but he wasn't in law enforcement and Duarte likely wouldn't tell him anyway. The important thing was, Zoe wasn't a suspect. "So she's free to go back to her life?"

Duarte nodded at him, then looked at Zoe. "Yes, but someone planted that knife and called in a tip that someone who looked like you was seen leaving Klein's residence. And since you can't think of anyone other than the deceased who would have done something like that, the killer's still out there. Framing you could have been an opportunity because Klein has enemies and you were an easy person to blame, or . . . his murder might have been an attempt to hurt you. You need to be careful."

"I will be," Zoe said, her arm wrapped around her mother's shoulders as she faced the detective.

After speaking to Blue and Mina for a few more minutes, the detective left the room. Zoe was still talking quietly to her mom and Sawyer felt suddenly awkward. He didn't want to leave Zoe but he knew she probably wanted to be with just her friends and family right now.

Sawyer cleared his throat and looked at Zoe. "I spoke to your boss and he was really understanding, but you probably want to call him and let him know you're okay."

"I will, thank you. Thank *all* of you," she looked around the room, tears welling in her eyes. "This is all so awful, I just can't..." She shook her head and wiped away the wetness tracking down her cheeks. Then she took a deep breath. "Dinner at my place tonight. All of you are invited. You too, Sawyer," she said, giving him a watery smile.

He just nodded as she continued.

"I'm sure Vincent will be back by this afternoon so I'll call—"

"I'll take care of calling your brother and sisters," Tanice said firmly. "And I'll make sure they don't hassle you for keeping us in the dark." She gave her daughter a firm squeeze around her middle, never taking her arm from around her daughter.

Zoe's eyes widened. "You will?"

"Yes. Sawyer explained why you felt the need to keep this a secret from us and I—" Her voice broke as she pulled Zoe into another hug, murmuring how thankful she was that Zoe was okay.

As Zoe hugged her mom, she gave Sawyer a grateful smile over Tanice's shoulder. The sight did strange things to his insides, just like when she'd given him that bright smile this morning. In that moment he realized just how easily he could fall for this woman if he wasn't careful.

CHAPTER FIVE

Zoe slipped into her room and shut the door behind her with a quiet click. She twisted the lock in case someone tried to come in because right now she needed just a couple minutes to herself. Voices and music from the living room and her back porch were a steady hum of activity.

She was so damn grateful to be here and surrounded by people she cared about and who cared about her in return, but today's events were finally crashing in on her and mental exhaustion crept through her veins, weighing her down. That third glass of wine probably wasn't helping her emotional state either.

When she heard running water coming from her bathroom, she straightened, that familiar tension punching through her—until Sawyer walked out.

He looked surprised, then almost sheepish to see her. He ran a big hand over his dark hair, his arm muscles flexing slightly with the movement. Her gaze trailed down the length of all those sinewy muscles. "There was a long line for your guest bathroom and I've had a couple beers. Figured I could sneak in here unnoticed and your mom said it'd be fine."

She stepped further into her room. It was weird having him in here, but she also kind of liked it and found herself thinking how good he'd look splayed out on her king sized bed. That thought was a jolt to her system. The man was gorgeous, but she hadn't thought lusting after someone would even be on her radar right now. "After what you did today, you don't have to apologize for anything, ever. My mom thinks you're a saint. Whatever you did to keep her sane at the police station, thank you." She sat on the end of her bed and fidgeted with the light blue and brown comforter. It still felt surreal that she'd been freaking arrested this morning and was now celebrating with friends and family since she was free and clear.

Half-smiling, he stepped closer, moving with that predator-like grace that made her entire body alert with awareness. Not only had he stepped up today and just taken over, calling everyone necessary, he'd been so sweet to her mom. It wasn't like he'd had to stay at the police station. Sure, he was insanely sexy, something she was finding impossible to ignore tonight. He had on dark slacks and a dark green sweater that made his piercing eyes pop even more against his tanned skin. The sweater sleeves were pushed up his forearms, showcasing muscles she wanted to trace with her fingers and lips. Looks aside, the man clearly had an honorable streak—and that was the sexiest thing of all.

He sat next to her, reaching out a hand as if to squeeze her leg, but pulled back at the last second and placed it on the comforter instead. There wasn't much space between them and she swore she could feel his body heat. His scent was purely masculine, subtle and made her think of springtime. Being this close to him sent a shiver of pure delight down her spine.

"How're you holding up?" he asked quietly.

"Great!" she said a little too brightly, then winced. "Okay, how fake did that sound?"

Sawyer's chuckle made butterflies take flight in her belly. "Pretty bad. It's okay to *not* be fine."

"I know, I just don't want anyone to worry."

"Well, you don't ever have to fake it with me," he said quietly.

God, this man. Her gaze dipped to his lips almost against her will. When he made a rumbling, sort of growling sound, her eyes snapped up to meet his. Pure fire simmered beneath the surface of his gaze as he watched her.

She sucked in a breath at the visible lust. Oh yeah, no denying that. Any other night under any other circumstances she'd have over analyzed this to death, like she always did, but not now. Not when her stalker was dead and she felt like she could get back to living her life, to feeling normal again. But she didn't want normal and boring. She wanted a taste of Sawyer.

Without thinking, she leaned forward and brushed her lips over his, softly. He stiffened slightly and she wanted to die of embarrassment. Maybe she'd made a mistake, misread the—

Sawyer crushed his mouth over hers, moaning into her mouth like a starving man.

She clutched his shoulders and suddenly found herself flat on her back on the bed, one of his thighs between her legs as they kissed. He was huge and she loved the sensation of being pinned down by all that raw strength. Kissing seemed like such a dull description for the way he was devouring her. She felt like she was a teenager again, making out for the first time, and that was insanely hot.

He tasted like coffee and chocolate, rich and sweet and she arched into him, sliding one hand down his back. She wanted to touch every inch of him. He held the back of her head in a solid grip as his other hand grasped her hip. He wasn't making a move to do anything else other than kiss.

Normal Zoe wouldn't make the first move, especially not with a man she'd only had a couple conversations with. Normal Zoe wouldn't even think about sleeping with someone she hadn't gone on at least half a dozen dates with, probably more. And by then she usually lost interest.

Normal Zoe could take a hike right now.

She slid her hands up the front of Sawyer's shirt, shoving at it, wanting to see and feel all of him. Every muscular inch he was trying to hide under his clothes. She felt almost crazed with the need.

When he pulled his head back, breathing hard, he stared down at her. "How much have you had to drink?"

"Not enough to regret this."

He started to respond, but she was having none of it. Reaching down, she grasped the edge of her fitted purple sweater and tugged it over her head. Before she'd pulled it all the way up Sawyer made a sexy-as-sin growling sound.

"Fuck," he murmured, his gaze tracking over her exposed chest and torso. "I was going to say this is too fast."

"You sure about that?" she murmured.

"I don't want to take advantage," he continued, his voice strained as he sat up, staring down at her as if he didn't know where he wanted to start.

Reaching behind her back, she unsnapped her black bra and let it slide down her arms as she sat half up. "Then let me take advantage of you." She had no idea where the bold words came from, but she felt as if she was on fire right now. New Zoe celebrated. A burning heat simmered inside her and was only growing hotter. The only thing that could ease her ache was Sawyer.

He made another strangled sound before his head suddenly dipped toward her breasts. She gripped his head, urging him on. He sucked on one hard nipple, palming the other with a surprising gentleness. The way his tongue laved over her sensitive bud had her arching into him, demanding more. She hummed with energy, as if she could crawl right out of her skin for how good he felt.

Gently, he pressed his teeth around her nipple and flicked his tongue over it, back and forth, as he rubbed his thumb over her other one. The dual sensations were making her crazy, heat building in between her legs like—

Knock, knock. "Zoe?" She froze at the sound of Vincent's voice.

Sawyer's head snapped up. "Is the door locked?" he whispered, not worry on his face, but clear discomfort.

She nodded at Sawyer as she called out, "I'll be out in just a sec, V."

"Okay, just making sure you're good. A couple people are asking about you, but take your time." He sounded so sweet and sincere, she had to smother a laugh. He wouldn't be telling her to take her time if he knew what she was doing in here.

Sawyer made an almost inaudible groan and laid his head against her breast bone. "We don't have enough time to do everything I plan to do to you anyway," he whispered.

She slid her fingers through his dark hair and bit back a groan of her own. Her entire body was primed for an orgasm but there was no way in hell they could finish what they'd started. She had guests anyway and just couldn't stay in here ravishing Sawyer, no matter how much she wanted that. But that didn't mean she wasn't disappointed. It was probably better this way though. Things might have gotten awkward—wait, what had Sawyer said? "Are you still planning on . . . doing those things?"

His head lifted and his eyes connected with hers, the intent in them clear. "Oh yeah."

A shiver rolled through her and she fought the sudden urge to kick everyone out of her house so she could find out exactly what he had planned. After the number her ex had done on her, she hadn't dated much in years—not that what she and Sawyer were going to do would be considered a date. Work had also prevented much of a social life so tonight she was going to make up for all those times she worked instead of having fun.

* * *

"Are you sure you don't want anything to drink?" Mallory Tate asked, twisting her slender fingers together in her lap.

"I'm good, but thank you," Detective Carlito Duarte said, briefly scanning her sparse living room. There weren't many personal touches and he knew she hadn't been living in the waterfront condo more than a month. "You've already been eliminated as a suspect so you can relax. I just want to know more details about your husband."

"*Ex*-husband." Then she seemed to remember herself and cleared her throat.

It was late Friday night but the woman had been willing to talk to him. Not that Carlito had given her much of a choice. He'd told her he could meet her now or bring her down to the police station for questioning. Since she'd already been questioned while her alibi was being confirmed he knew she had no desire to go back to the station.

"Sorry, *ex*. So tell me a little more about him. What he was like as a husband." Often it was better to let people just talk instead of giving them specific questions, especially in a situation like this. She was more likely to be honest this way.

"He was..." She looked behind him, her pretty face tensing for a moment before she met Carlito's gaze again. "I'm sorry, it's hard to believe he's dead."

"I'm sorry for your loss," he murmured, even though he wasn't sure he was sorry at all. Not after the report he'd read from Zoe Hansen.

"I'm not." Mallory's voice was so quiet he almost didn't hear her. In her late thirties, she had long, honey-blonde hair and long, lean limbs. She was conventionally attractive but there was an almost regal air about her. The type of women he so often came into contact with in Miami from the upper crust had a plastic quality about them. Not Mallory Tate. She was the kind of woman who would definitely age gracefully.

He raised an eyebrow. "I take it that it wasn't a happy marriage?"

"At first it was. Or I thought it was." She tucked a strand of hair behind her ear, her fingers trembling. For a brief moment he saw a flash of fear in her gaze, the type he'd seen on the faces of countless battered women before.

Well, hell. She'd never filed any reports and there'd been nothing in his measly information file on her to suggest Klein had abused her. She hadn't said much when she'd been at the station earlier, had let her attorney do most of the talking. "Nothing you say has to leave this room. Just let me know what's on the record and off."

His words seemed to trigger something in her because she straightened. "I don't care who you tell. I'm tired of being afraid of him. I . . . know people thought I married him for his money or status, but it's not true. I loved him. Well, the version of him he let me see when we were dating. His previous wife seemed so vindictive and he convinced me she'd say anything to keep us apart, that she just didn't want him to be happy. Now I wish I'd taken the time to listen to her, but I was just so blinded, so in love. He was very charming but about a year after our marriage that veneer started to crack. I won't bore you with details because I'm sure you've heard the same, tired story a hundred times before." She laughed, the sound brittle and self-deprecating.

"I want to hear your story." He meant it. After speaking with her at the station he thought he'd had her pegged. He'd been wrong. It didn't happen often.

She gave him a wry smile. "He changed, or I guess he just started showing his true colors. It was little stuff at first, nothing I did was good enough. Or I embarrassed him at a hospital function—which was complete crap considering he was the one who always got drunk, but that's not the point. At a fundraiser I caught him fooling around with a woman I know. We're not friends, but we belong to the same country club. I was angry and went to see a divorce attorney that week. I tried to leave him but . . . he made it clear I'd never be allowed to do that."

Bastard. "How?"

She swallowed hard and glanced down at her hands, clenched tightly together in her lap. For a moment he thought she wasn't going to answer. Then her voice came, quiet and sure. "He drugged me and raped me. More than once. He kept me drugged up for a week. I was too weak to fight him but I was aware of what he was doing the entire time. At the end of the week he broke one of my arms. He made it clear that if I tried to leave him again, my punishment next time would be worse."

Carlito clenched his jaw, anger pulsing through him. He was supposed to stay objective during all cases, but it was hard to care that Klein was dead. Everything he heard about the guy was bad, that being an understatement.

"From that point he started monitoring my spending, accounts, everything. It was like living in a prison, until . . . I can't know for sure, but he must have started seeing someone because he started paying less and less attention to me. It was a godsend. I was able to start siphoning money away and I was getting ready to run when he left on that medical trip overseas." She snorted at that, bitter amusement on her face.

No wonder she'd been glad to see him go. Only years of experience in law enforcement allowed Carlito to keep his expression impassive.

"He divorced me before he left and it was the best thing that ever happened to me. Like being released from prison. I heard about what happened to Doctor Hansen later, from a friend whose husband works at the hospital, and I believe every word of what she said that he did. Braddock has—had—a God complex in the worst way. He would have been ballsy enough to attack her at the hospital and think he could get away with it. What's worse, he *did*." She shook her head, disgust clear on her face.

After taking note of the names of the two women she'd mentioned; the one she'd caught her ex-husband with and the friend with ties to the hospital, Carlito talked with her for a few more minutes before letting himself out.

It wasn't case-breaking evidence, but it was a start. He was going to find out who'd killed Braddock Klein, and more importantly, who'd tried to frame Zoe Hansen for it.

CHAPTER SIX

Sawyer glanced up from scanning the news on his phone and set it on Zoe's island countertop as she walked into the room, a silky multicolored robe cinched loosely around her slender waist.

"Coffee," she rasped out, blinking blearily at him before stumbling to her one-cup maker.

He bit back a smile and waited for her to get what she clearly needed. Last night hadn't gone remotely how he'd hoped. After their scorching kiss, the party had gotten louder and busier and people had stayed until almost three. Finally Tanice had politely cleared everyone out because Zoe had been barely staying on her feet from exhaustion—and some drinks.

While he'd wanted nothing more than to pick up where they'd left off, Zoe had had a few more glasses of wine and a couple shots from friends so he'd carried her to bed. Clearly she was feeling the effects now.

"Oh my God," she muttered, after taking a sip of her coffee. "I haven't done shots since I was twenty-two. What was I thinking?"

He snorted. "That you weren't in jail."

She grinned and pulled out a seat next to him. "Well, there is that. I can't believe you're still here."

He lifted an eyebrow. "You're really surprised?"

"Yeah. I was clearly not able to, you know…" Her cheeks flushed prettily as she trailed off and raised her cup to her mouth.

A mouth he'd had plenty of fantasies about before he'd finally dozed off in her guest room. There'd been no way he could have left her last night, not after everything she'd been through.

"Thanks for tucking me in last night. That was sweet." Before he could respond her eyes widened and she softly groaned. "Does Vincent know you stayed over?"

Sawyer stilled at her question. Her brother was the last person he wanted to think about right now. "Would it matter if he did?"

"No. Not for the reason you're thinking. Or I think you're thinking. Gah, I need more coffee." Glancing down, she took great interest in focusing on her drink.

Nope, he was having none of that. Reaching out, he snagged an arm around her waist and tugged her onto his lap. She let out a yelp of surprise, but moved willingly, settling across his thighs as she turned to face him.

"I just don't want to explain to my brother about whatever is happening between us. I'm a grown woman, but he's still my brother. And you two have a history."

As long as she didn't want to hide him. "Fair enough. Why were you surprised I was still here?"

Her cheeks flushed again and he had to bite back a groan. Seeing her like that brought up thoughts of what she'd look like naked, face and body flushed from pleasure. "I just thought, well, you know."

"That I'd bail because we didn't fu—end up in bed together?" He was used to talking bluntly, but he didn't like the thought of what he and Zoe would hopefully share soon as simple fucking.

"Yeah?" She lifted her shoulders slightly.

His jaw tightened but he didn't respond. They didn't know each other well enough for him to be annoyed about her assumption, even if it rankled him. "Go out to dinner with me tonight?"

She blinked, probably from the sudden change in subject, but nodded, smiling softly. "I'd like that. And, not that I don't like this position but, if you get between me and my coffee this early in the morning, we might have words," she murmured, reaching out to grab her mug.

"Duly noted." His lips twitched as she took another sip of the hot drink then let out an orgasmic-sounding sigh. He couldn't believe she woke up looking so fucking sexy. Her hair was wild and curly even though she'd tried to tame it back into some sort of clip thing. It didn't matter, the corkscrews bounced everywhere. Visions played in his mind of what it would be like to see her hair around her face and shoulders as she rode him, her back arched and her breasts bared for him to hold, kiss, lick.

"So how did you end up working for Red Stone?" she asked after another sip followed up with one of those sexy sighs.

God, those sounds were making him hard. He shifted uncomfortably, hoping she didn't notice. He'd always been in control of his body. Except around her apparently. "It was sort of a perfect storm of things. I'd hit my twenty year mark in the Navy—"

"Twenty?" Her eyes widened then she winced. "Sorry, didn't mean to interrupt."

"Interrupt all you want," he murmured, tightening his grip around her. "And yes, twenty. I joined when I was seventeen so I'm thirty-seven, if that's your way of asking."

"I wasn't, but I was curious. So, it was a perfect storm…"

He grinned, loving the feel of her sitting on his lap, in his arms. This light banter with a woman was new territory for him. It had been years since he'd been in a relationship and even then, his last one had been all physical, something he hadn't realized until too late. "It was just one of those things. The job offer came in and I had to take it."

"You were in California for a long time though, right?"

He nodded. "Yeah. I wasn't home often but that's where I was stationed for the majority of my career."

"Do you miss it?"

San Diego was beautiful, but bases were pretty much the same wherever you went. And the Navy had been his home, not a city. "I miss my men and I miss the structure, but I'm adaptable. A nomad, my mom always says."

Zoe raised an eyebrow. "Your mom?"

"Well I wasn't spawned."

She snorted. "I just meant are your parents, or your mom, still alive?"

He nodded. "Yep. They run an alpaca farm in Missouri with two of my brothers. They're starting to downsize this year, but I don't know that they'll ever give it up completely."

"That's pretty interesting. So how many brothers do you have?"

"Four total." He loved all of them, but never could have stayed in Missouri. He'd wanted to see the world too much and the need to protect his country had been an almost inborn thing. There'd never been another option other than the military for him and he'd known it since he was a kid.

"Let me guess, you're the oldest."

He shook his head. "Middle child. What about you? Oldest?"

"Nope. Two older sisters and you know Vincent is the baby."

Sawyer snorted at that. "I'm sure he loves being called that."

A smile played on Zoe's full lips and she shifted slightly against his lap. When she did, her hip brushed right over his erection—and she froze, her expression turning to one of surprise.

"You're really surprised?" he murmured.

Her eyes grew heavy-lidded as she watched him. She shook her head and ran her tongue along her bottom lip, almost nervously as she set her coffee cup down.

He didn't bother fighting his groan as he watched her moisten that full lip. "What are you thinking right now?" he whispered.

Her gaze narrowed on his mouth and she leaned forward, gently brushing her lips over his. "What do you think?"

Sawyer didn't want to screw things up with Zoe by going too fast, but damn, the woman was making it impossible not to. When she playfully nipped his bottom lip between her teeth, he knew this was a battle he was going to lose because no way was he turning away from her. From this.

But he *was* going to take control of the situation. Wrapping his hands around her hips, he lifted her off him until she was sitting on the edge of the island. Her silky robe parted, revealing a light pink slip thing he was pretty sure was called a chemise. Her cheeks were flushed with arousal and he could see the outline of her hard nipples through her clothes.

Keeping his gaze on hers, he slowly slid a hand up her inner thigh. Her breath hitched, growing ragged, and he didn't stop until he teased the edge of her panties.

He couldn't see them yet, but his imagination was going wild as to what color they were. "I want to kiss you here," he murmured, cupping her mound as he leaned in to cover her lips with his. Her legs spread under his hold and he shifted so that he was perfectly in between her thighs. The blinds in her kitchen were still closed, but plenty of natural light streamed in through the cracks in the slats, letting him see her every expression.

She nodded and made a moaning sound he felt all the way to his cock. Touching her was making him crazy. Last night had been a tease of what was to come and now he wanted to see all of her.

When he feathered kisses down her jaw, she arched her back, letting her robe fall farther open. He slid it all the way off, letting it glide to the countertop without a sound.

Her fingers trailed over his chest as he made his way down to her shoulders, nipping at her skin. Impatient to see her breasts again, he pushed the straps down, letting the silky covering pool around her waist.

He had to pull back just so he could stare. Dark brown nipples and perfect, pert breasts just a little more than a handful. Her abdomen was flat and toned, as if she worked out or ran. "You are built for sin," he murmured, looking up at her as he spoke.

Her dark eyes glinted wickedly as she reached for the hem of his shirt. "I could say the same thing about you."

Instead of letting her do it, he tugged his shirt off then dipped his head to one of her breasts. Just like last night, she let out the sexiest moan, her back arching into him as she clutched his head with one hand, holding him close. Her other hand moved to his back, her fingers digging into his skin.

He could have stayed where he was all morning, teasing both her breasts, working her into a frenzy, but he wanted to taste between her legs, wanted to see how wet she was, to push her over the edge the way he hadn't gotten to last night. Reaching between them, he tugged off her panties—black Brazilian cut, he noted—and gently pushed her backward.

"Lay back," he ordered.

She paused, and he could tell this was a test for her. From the little time he'd known her he understood she liked to be in control. Right now, he hoped she'd let go. When she finally did, he bent down between her legs and sucked in a breath at the sight of her. Completely bare. Her skin was soft and smooth and just the hint of her clit was peeking out from her lips. "You wax?" he rasped out.

"Mm hmm." She shifted slightly, moving closer to the edge of the counter, as if nervous or maybe just anticipating.

Hell, he couldn't hold back any longer. Leaning down, he felt fucking barbaric as he inhaled her scent, wanting to imprint it in his mind. God, the woman was sweet. Everything about her. He slid his tongue up the length of her slit and didn't bother hiding his groan when she jerked against his face.

She moved her feet from the edge of the counter to his shoulders, digging her toes into him as he began teasing and licking. Each time he stroked against her slickness, she let out a strangled sound and arched herself right against his face.

When she tried to clamp her legs around his head, he pressed on one inner thigh and chuckled against her. At the motion, she jerked even harder than before, making his dick ache. He was going to slide into her soon, but first he desperately wanted to taste her release on his tongue. The need was damn near primal. He wanted to see her completely undone because of him, to see her lose control.

Right about now he wished he had four fucking hands because he wanted to touch her everywhere. As he slid a finger inside her, she grabbed onto his head, her inner walls clenching tight around him. All he could think about was how amazing it would feel to have that tightness wrapped around his cock. But first . . . He sucked on her clit, the action making her cry out in surprise and desire.

"Just like that." Her voice was a shaky whisper.

He could barely hear it over the sound of blood rushing in his ears. Years ago, he'd endured twenty-five weeks of BUD/s—the most intensive training in the world, and become a Navy SEAL. His skill set was vast, he could survive on pretty much any terrain on the planet and could navigate practically blind in the dark ocean. He had a sixth sense about things, as did most guys in special forces, but right now, if someone walked up behind him with a weapon, he wasn't certain he'd sense them coming because all his focus was on Zoe.

Her pleasure.

Her taste.

The sounds she was making with each stroke of his tongue.

The woman was making him insane, his erection pulsing insistently between his legs. He slid another finger inside her and she came apart underneath him, jerking and moaning incoherent words. Sucking harder on her clit, he increased the pressure when he could tell she liked it and started thrusting his fingers, in and out.

Each time he stroked inside her, her walls tightened harder and harder around his fingers as her orgasm punched through her, her toes digging into his back as her fingers did the same to his head.

When she fell limp against the counter, he slowly pulled his fingers out of her. With his gaze on her heavy-lidded one, he slid his fingers between his lips. It was like the action set something off inside her. Her eyes sparked with pure hunger.

No longer lax, she pushed up and grabbed for the buckle of his pants, her breathing erratic. *Yes.* As she worked it free, he pulled a condom from his back pocket. Before he could think about opening it, she snagged it from his hands and tore it open.

As she did, he shucked his pants, his erection springing free, a heavy club between his legs. When she sucked in a breath he saw her looking at his hard length, eyes wide. Just as quickly she grinned and reached for it, ready to roll the condom on.

He stilled her, grasping her wrist before she could. "Next time." Because he was on a razor's edge right now. He wanted to feel her gentle fingers wrapped around him, but he wanted her tight body even more.

Taking it from her, he quickly rolled it on, his hand shaking—actually shaking. The counter was too high, something she seemed to realize at the same time he did.

"Living room." Her voice was breathless as she reached for him, linking her fingers behind his neck and wrapping her legs around his waist.

He locked his arms around her and tugged her close, savoring the feel of her breasts rubbing against his chest as he crushed his mouth to hers. Teasing her lips open, he flicked his tongue against hers, her taste making him crazy.

From the party, he knew the layout of her house so he moved quickly across the tile—until she lifted up against him and impaled herself on him.

He sucked in a breath, his head snapping back from hers. Groaning as he filled her, she arched her back against him, her nipples stroking his chest with the movement. They weren't going to make it to the living room. "Wall or floor?" he managed.

"Wall." He loved that she didn't even pause in her answer.

He barely made it to the nearest kitchen wall before pulling out and thrusting back in, hard. Using the wall to brace them, he held onto her ass and began a steady rhythm, pounding into her. "Can you touch yourself?" he managed to rasp out. Because he wanted her to come again while he was inside her.

Her breathing was erratic as she reached between their bodies and started strumming her clit. It was insanely sexy that she was so comfortable with her body, the sight of her touching herself making him harder if that was even possible. His balls pulled up tight, the base of his spine tingling as the buildup increased. God, he was close. With her tight body wrapped around him like satin, it wasn't going to take long. Not this first time.

Dipping his head to hers, he kissed her again before blazing a path down her jaw to where her neck and shoulder met. He tilted her head to the side as he raked his teeth over her skin. When she shuddered he realized how sensitive she was there.

"Come for me," he murmured as he pulled out of her again, almost fully, before sliding back in with a groan. She was so damn tight. "I want to feel you coming on my cock."

It was like his words set something off inside her. Her breathing hitched and her inner walls, which had already been incredibly tight around him, started rippling. She buried her face against his neck and bit down lightly, groaning against him as she found another orgasm.

That was all he needed to let go. With a cry, he climaxed, emptying himself, thrusting into her over and over until he buried himself completely inside her sweet heat. Breathing erratically, he stayed where he was, not inclined to leave for a while.

Eventually she shifted against him, making a soft groaning sound. He managed to pull his head back from hers to find her looking completely sated, her dark eyes filled with warmth.

She grinned that smile that held the power to bring him to his knees. "We're so doing that again."

Hell yeah. "Are you on birth control?"

She nodded and he found himself grinning right back at her as he imagined sliding into her heat without a barrier. "Good." He was clean and figured they could have that conversation later but if she was on the pill he knew it wouldn't be long until they got to that point.

Slowly he pulled out of her and disposed of the condom. When he turned back from the garbage he found her sliding the silky straps of her nightgown back up her shoulders. In their haste she'd never taken it completely off, just let it pool around her waist.

Next time, it was coming off. He wanted all of her bared to him. "Are you hungry?" he asked, picking up his discarded pants.

"Starving," she murmured, stepping toward him. He pulled her into his arms, loving the way she leaned into him, kissing along his chest as she wrapped her arms around his waist. "Want to order something or head out? There's a cute little Cuban restaurant not far from here that serves breakfast."

Her curls tickled his nose as he kissed the top of her head. "I'll cook for you," he said. She had enough in her refrigerator he could easily whip something up for them.

"That's the hottest thing you've said all morning, and that's saying something." She groaned slightly as if she didn't want to pull away from him before snagging her fallen robe from the floor. As she did, her doorbell sounded. They both paused and a frown tugged at her lips. "I'll get it," she said when he went to go with her. "Seriously I've got my alarm set and I'll look through the peephole. It's probably just a neighbor."

Sawyer didn't like it but he also didn't want to come off as a domineering jackass and insist on going with her to answer the door. But . . . Fuck it. Technically he wasn't guarding her anymore via Red Stone, but that didn't mean he wasn't going to stop watching out for her. There was no way in hell he could just turn off this part of himself, not when it came to Zoe's safety. "I know you're capable of taking care of yourself but whoever planted that knife is still out there."

Zoe looked as if she wanted to argue, but just nodded. "It might be overkill but okay."

It went against all his instincts not to just take over and look through the peephole, but he let her go first. When the bell sounded again, she grumbled under her breath as they reached the door. Lifting up on her tip-toes, she looked through, then let out a real curse.

Her mouth pulled into a thin line as she looked at him. "It's Vincent."

Perfect damn timing. Sawyer looked down at himself and grimaced. "I'll put my shirt on," he said quietly, striding toward the kitchen as she disarmed her alarm system.

It was going to be awkward enough with him being here this early in the morning and he didn't think Vincent would appreciate seeing him half-dressed. Not that he really cared what the other man thought.

The only one whose opinion mattered was Zoe.

CHAPTER SEVEN

Before opening her front door, Zoe glanced in the mirror above her foyer table and winced. Her lips were slightly swollen, her cheeks flushed and her hair was a little out of control. Which wasn't exactly out of the ordinary but she released her hair from her clip and tried to finger comb the curls so she didn't look as though she'd just had sex against the wall. It was no use.

Setting the clip on the table, she took a deep breath and opened the door to find her brother there scowling. What was wrong with him? "Hey, Vincent. Kinda early for you to be here. Everything okay?"

"Is that Sawyer's truck in your driveway?" he demanded. He wore running shorts, sneakers and a long-sleeved Nike Dri-Fit shirt he loved so much, as if he'd planned to go jogging.

She didn't bother looking past him to see the offending vehicle. "Would you like to come in, have some coffee?"

Vincent just growled and stomped past her, his expression dark. "Where is he?"

"Seriously, on what planet do you think I'm going to let you come in here and go all caveman about my personal life?"

Vincent's pale blue eyes that looked so much like their deceased father's flashed angrily. "Personal life! You just had a big scare yesterday, Zoe. You're probably feeling emotional and vulnerable and he's taking advantage."

"Emotional and vulnerable? Okay, what happened to my brother? Because he doesn't use words like those."

His jaw tightened. "I'm serious."

"So am I. And I'm a big girl so if this is the only crazy reason you stormed over here this morning, then you can go right back the way you came. I appreciate your concern, but..." She trailed off when Sawyer appeared in the arched entryway of the dining room. The dining room was connected to the kitchen so he'd have heard everything clearly. She inwardly winced.

Silence stretched out as the two men stared at one another, Vincent's hostility seeming to grow each second that passed. She wasn't sure what to say that wouldn't set off her brother's normally long fuse. Before she could figure it out, Sawyer stepped farther into the foyer.

He held up his palms in that universal sign for peace. "Look, Vincent—"

"Is this about Audrey?" Her brother's voice rose with each word, his body vibrating with anger.

Sawyer's lips pulled into a thin line, his expression tense. She couldn't read what he was thinking other than he seemed annoyed by Vincent. "Are you kidding me?" His words were clipped.

"Who's Audrey?" Because she wanted to know whatever had happened between these two. It shouldn't surprise her that a woman was the reason for their past issues. Still, a strange sense of jealousy settled in her bones. After everything that had happened with her ex-boyfriend, she didn't like the sound of this.

They both ignored her.

Sawyer's expression was frustrated as he looked at Vincent. "You think it's impossible that I could be attracted to Zoe, a smart, beautiful woman?"

"No, my sister's a fucking catch, I just don't like you sniffing around her."

Okay, Vincent calling her a catch was kinda sweet, but what the hell? Sniffing around her, like what, she was a bone and Sawyer was a dog? Sweet Lord, this was ridiculous. "Vincent—"

"And I don't like your timing," Vincent continued, taking an angry step closer to Sawyer. They'd both been in the Teams but they'd never been on the same one as far as Zoe knew. Still, whatever had happened must have been bad for this kind of reaction from her brother.

"Timing?" Sawyer's jaw tightened and he took a step forward too. Not exactly menacing, but it was clear he wasn't going to back down to Vincent.

Uh, oh. She didn't think they were big enough jackasses to fight, not at their age, but . . . she stepped forward so that she was semi in-between them. Not that she could actually stop them if they decided to brawl.

Sawyer noticed her move and gave her an apologetic look.

Vincent still ignored her. "Yeah, timing. She's got all this shit to deal with then you just stroll in like a fucking knight in shining armor. What kind of game are you playing?"

"Oh my God! Vincent, enough!" Zoe stepped in between them fully now, hands on her hips as she faced off with her brother. She wished she was wearing more than a robe and slip and had on some damn heels so he didn't tower over her so much, but she'd never put up with his crap before and she wasn't about to start now. No matter how good his intentions were. Because she knew he was just looking out for her. Too bad he was going about it all wrong.

She held up a hand when it was clear he wanted to start his tirade on her. "Whatever this thing between Sawyer and me is, it's none of your business. *None.* I'm a grown woman—older than you. I actually can't believe you're here doing this." Vincent had never given her grief about any of the guys she'd dated in the past. Of course she'd never brought anyone around the family before, but still. The way he was acting was over the top and so unlike her brother. "It's not like Sawyer had anything to do with me having a stalker or said stalker being killed. We're attracted to each other, we're both consenting adults, get over it." He opened his mouth again, so she stepped forward and pressed a finger into his chest. "And if you say one word about me being vulnerable, like I haven't been handling this shit for the last six months all by myself, I will call Mom right now." It was the best threat she had.

Vincent's jaw tightened again, his pale blue eyes flashing fire. Finally he spoke again. "I know you're capable of taking care of yourself. I'm just not convinced Sawyer has your best interests at heart."

A sliver of worry wormed its way through Zoe. Vincent had never reacted about anyone like this. "Why's that?"

For a moment Vincent looked almost embarrassed or even ashamed. He scrubbed a hand over his face and sighed. "After Jordan left, I was in a dark place."

Zoe's entire demeanor immediately softened. When his now-fiancée had suddenly left him without a word seven years ago because she'd gone into WITSEC, Vincent hadn't handled it well. That being the understatement of the century. "Yeah, I remember," she said softly.

She still remembered when Vincent had confessed everything to her, how Jordan had just disappeared on him without a trace. Now he knew what had happened to her and they were a strong couple, but back then, he'd been a mess with her gone. Once he'd realized she'd left him, he'd lost it.

Vincent shot a quick look over her shoulder at Sawyer, then focused on Zoe again. "I slept with a woman he was seeing. To be fair, I didn't know they were together, but . . . after I found out, I was a dick about it to him."

"Jeez, Vincent." She frowned, wanting to cut him some slack, but it was hard to. If Vincent was actually admitting he'd been a dick, it must have been bad. And it sounded like Sawyer had more right to be pissed than Vincent about the whole incident. "Mom and Dad raised you better than that. *You're* better than that."

He held up his hands. "I know! It was a long time ago and that's not the point."

"So what is the point? You think because you did something douche to him that Sawyer is sleeping with me to what, get back at you?"

"You're sleeping with him?" His voice kicked up again.

She covered her face with her hands. "So *not* the point," she groaned before looking back at him. "You need to leave. Now." Because this was ridiculous and embarrassing. She was in her thirties and a professional, not someone trapped on a bad talk show—even though that was what it felt like at the moment.

Vincent looked incredulous. "You're kicking me out of your house?"

"Um, yes. Because this is childish." She narrowed her eyes at him as another thought occurred to her. "Does Jordan know you're here?"

He got that sheepish look she was very familiar with. "Not exactly. I told her I was going to grab breakfast—which I am."

Zoe snorted. "I bet she told you not to bother me about Sawyer."

That sounded exactly like Jordan. When she and Vincent had gotten back together Zoe hadn't been the nicest person to her because she hadn't known the circumstances of Jordan's disappearance. Now Zoe deeply regretted it. She hadn't been awful, but she *might* have called Jordan a bitch the first time they met. "You want me to call her *and* Mom? I'll do it."

"You're mean," he muttered. Vincent's lips twitched as if he was fighting a smile so she knew they'd be okay. He let out a sigh, shot Sawyer a dirty look that basically said 'this isn't over' before giving Zoe a kiss on the forehead and a hug and leaving.

Once he was gone she turned around, dreading to see Sawyer's face. Unfortunately his expression was that blank one she couldn't get a read on. He'd already been with her when she'd been arrested. Sure she hadn't done anything but he must think she was a drama magnet. "Sorry about that," she muttered.

"You don't have anything to apologize for." He still didn't reach for her, so she wrapped her arms around herself, feeling insecure. After everything they'd just shared it was like a chasm was growing between them and she couldn't stop it.

An awkward silence stretched between them. She wasn't sure what to say and maybe he wasn't sure either. Finally she decided to just ask the question. "Is there any truth to what Vincent said?"

If anything, Sawyer's expression became even more unreadable, and that was saying something. "You really have to ask that?" There was a bite to his words.

She realized he thought she meant the part about Sawyer possibly using her to get back at Vincent. "No, I just meant the whole thing that happened between you guys. Is that how it played out?" Because there was always more than one side to a story.

"More or less." His jaw tightened once before he continued. "I . . . loved her. We hadn't been together that long, but things were getting serious. Or I thought they were. Then she slept with Vincent—and threw it in my face."

Something told Zoe there was more to the story but right now, she didn't want to ask. It wasn't like she'd been expecting forever from Sawyer, but this cast a dark shadow on what they'd shared, whether it was fair or not. Her only serious boyfriend had still been in love with his ex when he'd been with Zoe. Something Zoe hadn't known until he'd dropped the bomb on her the day after they'd graduated from med school. Deep down she'd always wondered if Rubin hadn't gotten over his ex, but had never pushed it. She'd wasted two years with him.

She wasn't going to go through that again, not for anyone. "I'm sorry for what happened between you two and for what happened with your ex." She pushed out a breath. "Listen, a lot's happened in the past couple days and I've got a lot of stuff I need to do today. I know we were going to do breakfast but maybe we can take a rain check?"

She was simply feeling too raw to deal with him right now, even if her actions were unfair.

His jaw tightened as he watched her. "You shouldn't be alone right now. Whoever planted that weapon with your fingerprint is still out there."

"I know." The knowledge hadn't been far from her mind. But she couldn't cower and hide.

Blowing out a sigh that sounded a lot like frustration, he rubbed the back of his neck. It was clear he wanted to argue with her. "I don't like leaving you."

"I've got an alarm system, a gun and pepper spray." Not that she ever wanted to have to use either weapon.

There was a long, heated silence as he just watched her. Oh yeah, he did not like this at all. Before guilt completely suffocated her, he spoke. "You'll lock your doors and set your alarm when I leave?"

Gritting her teeth, she nodded. She didn't mind a little over protectiveness, but she could take care of herself. "I've got errands to run and stuff to do but I'll set it when I leave."

He paused and she guessed he was probably annoyed she'd be leaving her house, but seriously, she wasn't going to stop living her life. If she started down that path, she could get sucked into a life of fear and she refused to let anyone control her like that. "Are we still on for dinner tonight?" he finally asked.

"Yeah." The word was out before she could stop herself. She needed some time to herself, especially after everything that had happened the past couple days— months, really—but she still wanted to see him again. And she wanted to ask him about his ex, to find out if there was more to the story—if he still had feelings for the woman.

After he gathered his few belongings, she walked him to the front door and opened it. To her surprise, he pulled her tight against him, his big hands clutching her hips in a way that sent tingles straight to her toes.

And when he brushed his mouth over hers, stroking his tongue sensually against her lips, demanding entrance, she melted against him, holding his shoulders for support until finally she pulled back.

His breathing was uneven, his green eyes seeming darker as he looked down at her. "Tonight. Seven o'clock, I'll pick you up. And be careful."

"I will." Breathless from their kiss, she shut the door behind him and immediately locked it. He clearly wanted to see her again tonight, or she assumed he did. God, what if Vincent was right and he'd only made a pass at her because of—No. She wasn't going to let her mind go there. She wasn't going to obsess about him at all.

Not today when she had her freedom in more ways than one. She was going to do something she never did for herself—go to the salon and get the works done. Sawyer had left her feeling incredibly confused and if they were going out tonight, she was going to look like a million bucks when they did.

* * *

She wrapped her fingers around the hilt of her knife as she watched the tall man leave Zoe's home. He scanned the neighborhood, pausing at different intervals before finally he got into his truck and left.

She remained where she was, hiding in plain sight on the sidewalk across the street. She had one foot propped up against one of Zoe's neighbor's trees as she bent toward it, stretching. With yoga pants, a zip-up fleece hoodie and earbuds from her mp3 player in her ears, she looked like a mid-morning jogger, perfectly blending in with her surroundings.

So, Zoe had a lover? Or maybe this was a new boyfriend? The bitch had had a party last night when she should have been in jail. Instead she'd been celebrating that Braddock was dead. Of course she wouldn't have come out and said that was why she'd had the party, but it had to have been the reason. If it had been big enough, she'd have gone inside, but she hadn't been invited and while she knew Zoe, they weren't friends.

The whole situation wasn't right. Zoe should be suffering. It was her fault that Braddock was dead even if Zoe hadn't been the one to cut his throat. If he hadn't wanted Zoe so much, been so obsessed with the idea of her, then Braddock would have been with her. She could have made him forget that bitch.

But he'd been a fool, wanting what he couldn't have. So now he was dead and Zoe was next. Killing her would be tricky though, especially now. Since Zoe hadn't been arrested, the police must have figured out the doctor hadn't done it. Planting that knife with her fingerprint had been a long-shot, but it had been worth it. Unfortunately it hadn't worked out.

That was okay. Toying with Zoe would be so much more fun than just killing her. Once the truck was out of sight, she continued jogging, looping back around the neighborhood multiple times. On her third time around, she saw Zoe's car pulling out of her garage.

Her heart rate kicked up. Zoe was leaving. This was perfect. She knew the bitch had an alarm system, or she at least had stickers on her windows and a sign in her yard that said she did, so she wouldn't bother breaking in. No, she was going to leave Zoe a present for whenever she returned.

Her entire body heated up as she thought about the expression on Zoe's face when she found it. Unfortunately she wouldn't be around to see Zoe's horror, but she could still fantasize about it. Though it killed her, she didn't slow down as Zoe left, just kept jogging, kept her pace even. When she reached the end of the road, instead of looping back the way she'd come, she crossed the street and headed back down the sidewalk toward Zoe's house.

Once she reached it, she glanced around casually, keeping up that steady pace as she headed up the driveway then the stone walkway to Zoe's front door.

On the front step, she pretended to ring the doorbell as she pulled a small package out of one of her hoodie's pockets. Since it was so cold out she was wearing gloves and wouldn't look odd, which made this so much easier. She'd been careful not to leave any prints on the package or the wrapping.

The wrapping itself was a bright silver and green with little snowflakes on it. An early Christmas present for Zoe.

Laughing to herself, she set it right on the front stoop, propping it against the door. The present was small but the contents inside would be very effective.

It was just a shame she wouldn't be able to see Zoe's face when she opened it.

CHAPTER EIGHT

Zoe shut one of her desk drawers and looked up as Gerard stuck his head in her office.

His mouth pulled into a frown. "What are you doing here?"

She held up her hands in mock self-defense. "Not working, I swear. Just had to pick up a few things." She'd gone to the salon and felt like a new woman. She was about to head home but had needed to stop by work first.

He leaned against the door frame and stuck his hands in his pants pockets. "Hair looks good."

"Yeah?" Zoe self-consciously ran her fingers through it. She'd had it straightened for a little change. Once she washed it, the curls would return but she'd wanted something different for the next couple days. Almost like a cleansing of all the drama from her past—and if she was being completely honest with herself, she wanted to look amazing for Sawyer.

"Why the change?"

She narrowed her eyes at him. "I thought you said it looked good."

"It does. But . . . something's different about you."

Her cheeks flushed as she thought about what she'd done this morning with Sawyer, then she cursed herself. It wasn't like Gerard could read her mind. "I have no idea what you're talking about."

He started to say something but was cut off by a familiar female voice. "Gerard?"

Zoe rolled her eyes but Gerard just sighed. Viola, tall, willowy and beautiful, the physician's assistant had been crushing on Gerard for a while and couldn't seem to take a hint that he wasn't interested. It had placed him in a weird position and Zoe knew he was starting to feel uncomfortable about the woman's attention. Zoe understood all too well what that felt like since her stalker had been like that with her.

"Want to head out with me?" Zoe murmured quietly. Before he could answer, Viola appeared in the doorway.

She gave Zoe a tight smile that didn't reach her eyes.

Well the feeling is mutual, Zoe thought. At least the woman was good at her job, very organized, one of her only redeeming qualities.

Without giving Zoe another glance she turned to look at Gerard, already crowding his personal space as she leaned closer, practically shoving her breasts at him. "What are you two doing here? I didn't think you came in on Saturdays, Zoe," she said, still looking at Gerard. There was an almost accusing note in her voice.

Zoe didn't bother answering. Just locked her top drawer as Gerard cleared his throat. "Just catching up on some paperwork, but we're heading out now." He gave Zoe a pointed look.

She resisted the urge to smile as she slipped her coat on. "Yeah, Gerard owes me dinner." A complete lie but she had no problem covering for him.

Viola frowned and glanced at her slim, silver watch. "This early?"

"Gerard likes to get the early bird specials. Especially at his age." Zoe snickered now, unable to contain her laughter.

He just shot her a dirty look as Viola's pink-painted lips pulled into a frown. She stroked a hand down his forearm, an action that could be considered casual, but the possessive glint in her eyes was anything but. "I'm heading out to get some drinks before dinner with friends in a couple hours. Do you guys mind if I tag along?"

Zoe couldn't think of a polite way to say no. Viola might annoy her but she couldn't be all out rude to her. It was weird that she'd stopped by the office though when clearly she hadn't done any work since she'd just arrived. Good Lord, was she really here simply to see Gerard?

"Of course not," Gerard said smoothly and Zoe want-ed to kick him as she stepped toward them. She didn't even want to go to dinner, not when she had plans with Sawyer in a couple hours.

They both moved back and she shut her office door and started down the hallway with them. As they walked, Viola continued chatting. "So where are you guys going?"

"We haven't decided yet—"

Zoe was cut off when Gerard let out a frustrated curse.

"What's wrong?" Viola asked as they reached the front door.

"Nothing. Just an issue with my sitter," he said, looking at the screen on his cell phone. Which hadn't buzzed or dinged. His expression was apologetic as he looked between the both of them.

Zoe knew he was just pretending that he'd received a text, but Viola seemed to believe him. The woman made a lame excuse why she couldn't have dinner with Zoe and hurried toward her car as Zoe and Gerard locked up.

"Guess she didn't want to have dinner with just me," Zoe murmured.

He scrubbed a hand over his face after locking the door. "I don't know what to do about her. I've been careful not to be alone with her, but..."

"But you can't keep working like this. Sit down and talk to her and if that doesn't work, let her go."

"Yeah, I'm going to. I want you in on that meeting though."

Zoe nodded. "We'll record it too." Because she wanted to make sure her all her boss's bases were covered in case Viola tried to accuse him of something. Zoe wished he'd just fire the woman but knew Gerard would try to make things work first.

"How're you feeling after . . . everything?" he asked as they headed to their vehicles.

She shrugged, not sure about anything at the moment. Zoe didn't want to say out loud that she was glad her stalker was dead, but she was certainly happy she wasn't looking over her shoulder anymore. At least not because of Klein. It still freaked her out that a weapon with her fingerprint had been planted at the murder scene. Luckily she'd had a strong alibi. "The whole thing is still surreal. Last night was fun though."

He snorted. "I saw that. What time did everyone finally leave?"

"Three o'clock."

He let out a low whistle. "Apparently I really am a senior citizen."

"Whatever. You left at a normal time. I can't believe how late everyone stayed."

"What about your friend Sawyer? How late did *he* stay?" Gerard's look turned speculative as they reached his Lexus SUV. Grinning, he pressed the keyfob to unlock the doors, waiting for her answer.

"Why do you ask about him?" Zoe didn't think they'd been obvious last night. Not that she cared what anyone thought. She was single and could do whatever she wanted.

"The man couldn't take his eyes off you last night and something is really different about you this morning. Besides the hair."

"I'll let you know if anything interesting develops between us." She considered Gerard one of her closest friends but didn't want to tell him more about Sawyer until she knew where things were headed between them.

"All right. Just don't…" He trailed off.

A cool breeze blew up over the parking lot and she tightened her coat belt, fighting off a shiver. "Don't what?"

Gerard lifted his shoulders. "Maybe don't push him away or come up with reasons he won't work out?"

She started to defend herself, to insist that she didn't do that, but bit her bottom lip. Damn it, she did *exactly* that. Pretty much all the time. Sighing, she shook her head. "You're annoying when you're right."

He just chuckled, his breath a faint cloud in front of him as he gave her a brief hug.

Once she was on her way home, her boss's words rolled around in her head. Gah, she did push people away. Men at least. Relationships were so much work and took up so much damn time that she just couldn't fit one into her schedule.

At least that's what she told herself whenever someone asked her out. For years she'd just gone out with men who she considered low maintenance. Men who were in a profession similar to her own and therefore worked insane hours and were okay with her limited involvement in their lives. And vice versa. Ugh, thinking about it in those terms was depressing.

After Rubin left her she'd taken it hard. Harder than she'd admitted to anyone, even her brother, who'd been open about his own heartbreak years ago. It had been too much to admit that she hadn't been enough for her ex. On paper they'd been the perfect couple. Smart, successful, attractive people in the same field with the same views on politics and religion.

Okay, now *that* was depressing as hell too. Those things were important but she'd seen what her parents had. Their marriage hadn't been perfect but their love for each other had been. And they'd disagreed on all sorts of things, especially religion and politics. Her father had left a lush lifestyle to marry her mother. His wealthy, elitist parents had been blinded by anger when he'd fallen for a poor, black Jamaican, second-generation

American. Zoe wasn't sure what they'd hated more, her mother's skin color or her status as a resident. Not that it mattered to her or any of her siblings. Zoe hadn't talked to them in years. They'd reached out a few times after her father's death, but she couldn't be bothered with them. She'd seen what a good marriage was supposed to look like, what a loving family meant and she wasn't going to let those assholes into her life. Not when they'd flat out rejected her mom. Screw them.

As she steered into her driveway, she mentally shook herself, knowing exactly why she was thinking about her parents' marriage. She pressed her garage door opener but didn't pull through when she saw something shiny sitting on her front stoop. Getting out of the car, she hurried along the stone steps, her breath catching in her throat at the next gust of cold that rolled over her.

Smiling when she saw a small gift sitting there, she scooped it up. Probably something from one of the neighbors. Next weekend they'd be doing their annual gift exchange and party. Thankfully this year she wasn't hosting it at her house.

As she headed back to her car, movement from out of the corner of her eye caught her attention. Zoe hid a wince before she let her true feelings show. Letty Nieves was the same age as her and a beautiful woman.

She was also one of the most annoying neighbors Zoe had ever had. Zoe pasted on a smile, thankful her sunglasses covered her eyes, as the woman approached.

Wearing black yoga pants, a black long-sleeved T-shirt and a bright pink puffy vest zipped up over it, Letty smiled as she jogged up the driveway, though the smile was more of a baring of teeth—like a shark. "Hey, Zoe. Everything okay over here? I saw the police here yesterday."

And there it was. Letty was going to pretend she hadn't heard from the neighbors what was going on. "Everything's good. Getting ready for Christmas? Your light show is great this year." Zoe was the queen of avoiding and deflecting. She'd spoken to a few neighbors about what had happened, but Letty wasn't one of them. And she wasn't going to be one of them.

The tall woman with dark hair gritted her teeth, her smile growing sharper. "Thanks. I put a lot of work into it. You're sure everything's all right?"

"I'm sure."

Letty's gaze narrowed on the gift in Zoe's hand for a moment before she looked at her face again. "Saw a lot of people over here last night."

"Oh, yeah, just some people from work and family friends. Last minute get together type of thing." Zoe inwardly cringed. Maybe she should have invited Letty? No, last night had been a celebration and she hadn't wanted to have anything ruin that. And it wasn't like she'd invited the whole neighborhood or anything.

"Okay, well, let me know if you need anything. I'm here for you." Her voice dripped with a saccharine sweetness that raked over Zoe's senses.

Seriously, she had no idea why this woman didn't like her. She figured Letty was just one of those women who didn't like other women.

Whatever, Zoe didn't have time to worry about that now. Once she was securely inside her house, she reset her alarm and dropped her purse and coat onto the center island in her kitchen. She wasn't even going to pretend she could wait to open the gift.

Carefully peeling back the delicate paper, she opened it without tearing any of it. As she lifted the top of the small gold box off, it took a moment to register what she was seeing.

Her stomach lurched and she automatically dropped the square top. It fell to the counter with a soft click. A Polaroid of a gruesome scene—Klein's dead body, his throat slashed, blood sprayed all over his lanai—

The photo was covering . . . something underneath it. She could just see the tip of what looked like . . . No. It couldn't be.

Swallowing the bile in her throat, she grabbed a pen from her desk on the other side of the kitchen. Chills skittered up her spine that had nothing to do with the cold as she carefully moved the picture out of the way.

A severed finger with dried blood on the stump was nestled on a bed of white stuffing paper.

She wondered if it was Klein's finger or someone else's. Klein was clearly dead as that picture showed so who the hell could have done this? Grimacing, she pulled her cell phone out of her purse and called the police.

CHAPTER NINE

Sitting half inside the front passenger seat of Carlito's police-issued SUV, Zoe wrapped her arms tighter around herself. Her legs were half out of the vehicle as she sat sideways, taking in the scene in front of her.

Still trying to process the fact that someone had sent her a finger, probably Klein's, though it hadn't yet been confirmed, and that horrific photo was going to take time. She kept racking her brain, trying to figure out anyone in her life who could have done this. She came up blank. Once Klein had started stalking her she'd done research on the stalker mindset and knew that stalkers were often someone in your life. Definitely not always so this could be random, but . . . it felt *really* personal.

"Have you already talked to Vincent?" Carlito asked as he approached the vehicle, tucking his cell phone back into his jacket pocket.

She slid out of the SUV and nodded. "Yeah. I called Vincent and my mom and they're going to let my sisters know. My mom's actually going to stay with one of my sisters for a few days. And everyone is going to stay locked down in their houses tonight." Just in case whoever had targeted her decided to go after her family.

Carlito snorted. "Bet Vincent didn't want to."

Despite the situation, a grin tugged at her lips. "No, but he's got Jordan to look out for and you're here. He knows I'll call him when I leave and that I'll be getting a police escort to his place." Even though she really didn't want to go stay with her brother and Jordan. Not because she didn't love him, but they were newly engaged and planning a wedding. Zoe didn't want to get in the way of all that. For a brief moment she'd entertained the idea of calling Sawyer but things were new between them and she wasn't going to ask to move in with him—that would be insane. Plus she was really unsettled by her growing feelings for him.

"Did you finish the list of people—" He glanced to his left, frowning for a moment, then pulled out his radio.

She followed his line of sight. Police cars and two fire trucks lined the front of her house, blocking off most of the street. She'd always thought it was strange that fire trucks came to the scene of crimes but didn't care now. Red and blue lights flashed intermittently, creating the perfect 'crime scene' atmosphere. Zoe couldn't see whatever it was that still had Carlito frowning.

Gah, she rubbed her hands over her face. She just wanted to get out of here.

"It's some of your neighbors, they're across the street and want to talk to you, make sure you're okay." There was a questioning look in Carlito's gray eyes, as if he would let her go talk to them.

Zoe shook her head. "I'll call them later." She really appreciated their support but didn't have the energy to see anyone else now. Her house had been searched by the police even though as far as she knew no intruders had been inside, and she'd answered a hundred different questions.

"We're almost done here." He started to say more but his phone buzzed in his hand. Turning away from her, he said, "Yeah? Okay, yeah, he's good. I called him." Ending the call, he faced her again.

Zoe leaned against the side of the SUV, counting down the seconds until she could get inside her house. "I finished the list of people who I've ever had any sort of issue with in the last year. It's all there," she said, nodding to the open passenger door of the SUV where the pad and paper were. "I can't really see any of them doing this though."

"You'd be surprised," he murmured.

Before she could respond, Sawyer appeared from behind one of the fire trucks. She pushed up from the vehicle and was surprised when Carlito waved him over.

The expression on Sawyer's face was almost angry. But that couldn't be right. Why was he even here? She'd texted him to cancel their dinner plans tonight and had planned to call him once she was free and explain what was going on.

"Thanks for coming," Carlito said as Sawyer approached.

Though it was impossible, as he came to stand next to her, she could swear she felt his body heat wrapping around her. Wait—her head snapped back to Carlito. "*You* called Sawyer?"

The detective nodded, but his attention was on Sawyer. "I've gotta take care of something but I'll be back in a few minutes."

A couple uniformed police officers were in the nearby vicinity, hovering by Carlito's SUV, but all Zoe's focus was on Sawyer as the detective left them alone. "I'm confused, Carlito called you?"

"Yep." Sawyer's jaw was clenched tight as he raked a gaze over her from head to toe. The look was completely clinical—mostly. "You're sure you're okay?" Real concern laced each word as he met her gaze again.

Feeling unnerved by his presence, Zoe shoved her hands in her jacket pockets. The thick, winter coat had a fleece lining, warming her hands immediately. She hadn't called Sawyer for a reason. He'd already been witness to so much happening to her, she didn't want him getting even more tangled up in this mess. "I'm good. I just don't understand why Carlito called you."

"What I don't understand is why you *didn't.*" There went that sexy jaw clench again. The man was definitely angry.

At her.

"You're mad at me?" she blurted.

"Hell yeah, I'm pissed." He took a deep breath and glanced around their surroundings, as if trying to contain his anger. When he looked back at her again, all she saw was a simmering annoyance.

"But why? I was going to tell you everything once I got over to Vincent's house." Because no way was she staying here tonight. And she'd planned to give Sawyer a watered down version.

Reaching out, as if unable to stop himself, he ran his hands down her arms before pulling her close to him. A shudder slid through her, his presence warming her from the inside out. "Why didn't you call me about this? I would have been here."

Oh, crap. That was hurt in his voice. Which was way worse than anger. "I . . . didn't think you'd want to come down here for any of this. You've already done so much, I just..." She trailed off, feeling lame and guilty even though she'd never meant to hurt him. They might have had intense sex earlier that day but they weren't in a relationship. She didn't expect him to take on any more of this nightmare. It would be unfair to ask him.

Sawyer was silent, watching her with green eyes that seemed darker tonight. Instead of responding, he pulled her into a tight hug, wrapping his arms around her. She didn't even hesitate, but leaned into him, holding him tight. God that felt good. He'd come here to be with her, something that struck her deeply. She just wanted to get wrapped up in the strength of him and never let go—and that terrified her.

"How're you doing, really?" he asked quietly.

"It was awful." Her voice cracked, her words coming out muffled against his chest.

He rubbed a soothing hand down her spine, helping ease some of her tension. Not much but enough that she didn't feel like she was about to split apart at the seams.

"Come away with me for a few days," Sawyer murmured, his chin resting on the top of her head.

Surprised, Zoe pulled back so she could look up at him. "What?"

He fingered some strands of her hair before sliding his hand around to cup the back of her neck. "Instead of going to your brother's place. Let's get out of town. I know somewhere we can go. You can get some distance—which I think you need after Klein's death and your arrest anyway—and take a fucking break. The police can do their job and you can actually rest. Unless you really want to stay with your brother?"

The truth was, she didn't want to be around her family because she didn't want to inadvertently put any of them in danger. She knew they'd never worry about that because family was family and she'd feel the same if one of her siblings was in trouble. But . . . getting out of town sounded perfect. Still, she couldn't ask that of Sawyer. "You just started a new job."

"I know." His intense gaze never wavered.

She didn't know how to respond to that. He couldn't take off time right now. Or he shouldn't. And she wouldn't ask that of him. But his offer touched her on such a deep level it left her speechless for a moment. She must mean more to him than just hot sex, right? Or maybe he was just that honorable and didn't want to turn his back on someone in trouble. She bit her bottom lip, feeling way too indecisive.

Before she could respond, Carlito returned. "We're clearing out of here now. They've dusted the place for fingerprints just in case, but after the party you had, I doubt we'll get much. And there's no evidence he or she was ever inside anyway, but I want to cover all bases. Zoe, whatever's going on here is fucking personal. It's why I called Sawyer. Everyone in your life needs to be aware of this. And it wouldn't hurt for you to get out of town. I know you're going to Vincent's, but—"

"We're heading out of town tonight," Sawyer said, his voice commanding.

"Good. I've got a list of everyone you work with, the hospital staff you and Klein both worked with, your personal list and some other names we're going to be looking into. We *are* going to find this person but if you get out of Miami, I'll sleep easier." A harried-sounding male voice came over his radio, dragging his attention away again. He gave them an apologetic look and held it up to his mouth as he strode a few feet away.

"We're leaving tonight?" Zoe's eyebrows lifted as she turned to face Sawyer.

"Yes."

"Did you plan on asking me?" She wished she could put some heat behind the question but she was all out of steam. And the idea of getting away with him for a few days sounded like heaven.

Sawyer didn't back down, his expression hard. "Can you take time off work?"

"Yeah." Gerard wanted her to take off anyway. Once he heard about this, he'd likely pull rank and insist.

"Then no, I'm not asking." He glanced around, then lowered his voice before focusing on her again. "One of my brothers has a beach house in Saint Augustine. It's safe and not linked to either of us. We can be there in five hours."

"You're very bossy," she muttered.

"Where your safety is concerned? Yeah." His expression was like granite, hard and unforgiving.

"Wait, what about your job? You can't just take time off when you just started."

"It's not an issue." His voice was clipped.

"Sawyer—"

"Trust me. It's not."

She knew she should probably be annoyed by his tone and high-handed manner. She'd never put up with that from anyone before. Otherwise she wouldn't have gotten to where she was in life. But if she was being honest, it was nice to let someone else take over right now. And not just anyone, but Sawyer. She might still have no clue where they were headed relationship-wise, but she trusted him with her life. And the idea of leaving the city was so appealing, the answer fell from her lips without pause. She just hoped he wasn't putting his job in jeopardy. "Okay."

Normally she analyzed stuff to death, but not with Sawyer apparently. It was like he'd brought out a different side to her.

He nodded once. "Good. I've got a call to make then we'll talk to Carlito about where we're headed."

"I need to call Gerard too." Everything was happening so fast and she hated that she'd have to pass off some of her appointments, but she was terrified to stay home right now.

* * *

Across the street from Zoe's house, she blended into the shadows, careful to keep her body language neutral. She didn't want the glee on her face to show. Not that anyone was paying attention to her right now. She looked just like any other woman out for an evening stroll, curious about the police presence in such a quiet neighborhood.

She'd only gotten to see Zoe briefly when the bitch had been talking to a uniformed police officer. It wasn't enough. She wanted to see Zoe suffer, to see her expression of pain and fear. Just the thought made her entire body heat up with glee. A feeling similar to arousal swept through her. Her nipples pebbled against her bra and she shifted against the sidewalk, her sneakers silent on the concrete.

The more she thought about messing with Zoe, the more joy it brought her. That bitch deserved it more than she'd ever know. She just took and took and thought she could have anything she wanted. *Anyone* she wanted. Well, no more.

When a sexy-looking man in casual slacks, a jacket, and a police badge on a chain around his neck strode out from behind an SUV and waved at another man, her heart rate kicked up a notch. She recognized the man approaching the policeman.

Tall, muscular, dark hair, a hardness about him that was impossible to deny. He was definitely sexy, in a rough-looking sort of way. Not her type, she liked her men polished, but she could see the appeal. It was the man Zoe had been with before. Now he was here? Oh yes, he must mean something to her.

Probably here to support poor, pitiful Zoe. Too bad no one would be able to protect her for very long. It didn't matter where Zoe went, she had a way to track her. There was nowhere she could run. And if her lover got in the way, she'd end him too. Maybe she'd hurt him anyway and make Zoe watch.

CHAPTER TEN

Carlito sat on the edge of the seat in Letty Nieves's kitchen. Another uniformed police officer was with him, standing near the door that led into the backyard. Zoe had given them a list of people in her life who she didn't get along with. Since the Nieves woman lived in her neighborhood, he was starting with her.

It made it easier to pretend that he was just asking everyone in the neighborhood questions instead of subtly interrogating her. "Thanks again for agreeing to speak with us. Everyone in the neighborhood has been so helpful."

She smiled in a way he'd seen far too often, openly flirty. "Of course, Detective."

He bit back a sigh even though he could use this to his advantage. He'd used charm on many occasions to get suspects to loosen up. "Have you seen anyone around the neighborhood who looked out of place lately? Odd hours of the day or night?"

Letty shook her head, her dark hair swishing around her shoulders. In her thirties, she was a stunning woman, but something about her was plastic. "Not that I can think of. Well, yesterday I saw the police at Zoe's house, but I'm sure you already know that." There was a questioning note in her voice.

Deciding to be civil, he said, "Zoe's helping us with an ongoing investigation."

The woman's smile turned brittle, but she quickly recovered. "That's wonderful."

"Can you tell me about the rest of your neighbors?" Sometimes it was best to ask open-ended questions. People tended to hang themselves if given enough rope and in general, people loved to hear themselves talk. He hoped that was the case with Letty Nieves. So far he didn't have a gut feeling about her one way or another. It was too soon to tell. If she wasn't involved, hopefully she'd seen something that could help them.

"Of course." She clasped her hands in her lap and told him about both neighbors on either side of her, two across the street, and finally she got to Zoe. He had the feeling she'd been holding off on talking about Zoe when Letty's face tightened just a fraction as she mentioned her. "Now, I'm sure Zoe is helping you with your little case, but she's not the best neighbor."

Carlito straightened at that. "How so?"

She leaned forward, almost conspiratorially. "Trash comes on Thursdays early in the morning. *Before* she leaves for work. And she doesn't bring her trash can in until after she gets home."

He blinked, waiting for more. When he realized nothing more was coming, he fought his disappointment. This woman didn't like Zoe but it seemed to have more to do with her as a neighbor. He was sure people had killed for less, but after hearing Letty complain about every single one of her neighbors, she just seemed like an unhappy woman in general. He cleared his throat. "I see."

"And it's not just that. Last year she didn't take her Christmas lights down until January tenth. *Tenth*. Everyone else had them down a couple days after Christmas or by the first at the latest. Zoe was apparently too busy with her job." The woman sniffed haughtily and continued complaining about how Zoe's gardener had once left a tool in her front yard.

Carlito resisted the urge to massage his temple. He didn't have time to be a personal sounding board for this woman. When he'd been on patrol he'd gotten calls for the most ridiculous things; people called the police because their cable went out or because they wanted him to tell their eight-year old he'd arrest them if they didn't go to school. Because that wasn't going to scar them or anything. He'd thought when he became a detective it would be different, but nope. People were the same.

He smiled wanly and glanced over at the female officer standing guard. It was clear she was fighting a smile as she glanced out one of the kitchen windows to avoid his gaze.

Carlito cleared his throat again, and attempted to get back on topic. He needed to wrap up this conversation and move on to the next person on Zoe's list. Because whoever had left that finger for her to find was incredibly dangerous and he wanted them off the streets.

* * *

Sawyer steered into the driveway of the quiet beach house, using the high beams to sweep the front yard and foliage on either side of the home. Not for Zoe's current threat, but any threat. It was close to two in the morning and this house was unused about six months out of the year. Luckily his brother had someone who came by and cleaned bi-monthly and just checked on the place but still, he was more alert and vigilant than normal right now.

That 'gift' Zoe had been left was incredibly violent. Which said all it needed to about the person who'd left it. When he pulled up under the house, he inwardly cursed that they didn't have an enclosed garage. None of the houses on the water did though, because of hurricanes.

As soon as he turned off the engine, Zoe jerked awake, her eyes popping open, a tinge of fear visible in them, even under the muted moonlight. Her breathing was slightly erratic but quickly evened out as she gave him a nervous half-smile. "We're here?"

He nodded, his gaze raking over her for what felt like the hundredth time in the last few hours. She'd fallen asleep two hours into their drive and even before that she hadn't been much for conversation. It was clear she was scared and he'd wanted her to get some rest. He was going to make sure she felt safe tonight. If she let him, he knew exactly how he was going to help her take her mind off things. "Let me grab our bags and we'll head in. My brother texted me a couple hours ago, said we'd have the basics like milk and orange juice but later this morning we'll go grocery shopping."

Zoe gave him a real smile. "As long as there's a soft bed, I don't care about food."

At the word bed, all he could envision was her splayed out under him, her hips lifting to his mouth the way he'd been fantasizing about. That one time against her wall wasn't nearly enough. It had been raw and frantic and he wanted a whole lot more, especially after he'd gotten a taste of her. The woman could easily become an addiction, something he didn't mind.

For now he shut that thought down and quickly got out of the vehicle. After retrieving both their bags from the back, he led her out of the open garage and up the stairs to the next level. Like most houses on this stretch of beach front property, they were all raised at least fourteen feet higher than sea level. The stairs led to the wraparound porch and front door. As they ascended it, a cold breeze from the ocean whipped over them.

He heard Zoe make a shivering sound behind him and hurried to unlock the front door. Once inside he disarmed the code—his parents' anniversary date—then reset it and secured the door. "Tomorrow I'll show you around the house and we'll explore the beach."

She nodded, glancing around the foyer and connected living room curiously.

"You want the tour of the house now?"

She lifted a shoulder. "Yeah, I'd kind of like to know the layout of where we're staying in case . . . Well, in case of anything."

His eyebrows raised at her line of thinking. He'd be here to protect her, but he found her awareness of her surroundings fucking hot. Nodding to their left, he said, "This is the living room." His brother's wife had decorated the place in soft earth tones and most of the art anywhere in the house were black and white photos of ocean life or the beach. A giant ship's wheel hung above the fireplace, with other nautical-themed trinkets on the shelf under it. The tour of the house was as quick as possible with the living room, dining room, kitchen and office downstairs and four bedrooms upstairs. The place was huge for a beach house.

Once they reached the last bedroom, the master suite, he said, "You can take this one. It's big with a lot of privacy and your own bathroom."

She blinked, seemingly surprised by his offer. "Are you sure?"

He'd been hoping she'd ask him to join her but... "Yes. You've been through a lot. Plus I'll hear anyone coming up the stairs. No one will make it to your room without getting through me."

At his words, she wrapped her arms around herself and swallowed hard. Her newly straightened hair was windblown and tousled around her face from their short walk up the stairs. Right now she looked impossibly beautiful and scared. Shit. Maybe he shouldn't have said anything.

"Not that anyone's going to find us here." Screw it. He'd been trying to maintain distance between them because it seemed clear that was what she wanted, but he wasn't going to bother anymore. Not comforting her went against his nature and she clearly needed it. Besides, he hated the invisible wall she kept trying to put between them. He crossed the hardwood floor to where she hovered near an oversized trunk at the end of the king-sized bed. When he went to place his hands on her hips, to pull her close, she set a hand on his chest and shook her head.

"Don't."

That one word made him freeze. "Don't what?"

"Touch me right now." Her voice cracked on the last word before she swallowed hard again. "If you do, I'll invite you to join me in bed and I don't think that's the smartest thing right now."

"Why not?" he asked bluntly. Because getting naked with her sounded like a damn fine idea.

Her eyes widened at his question. Clearly he'd taken her off guard. She nervously cleared her throat. "Well, it's just not. After everything that happened with you and my brother and then with me being targeted by some maniac, I don't know. Sleeping together just doesn't seem like a good idea right now."

It was clear she was grasping at straws. The shit that had gone down with her brother was long-buried and had nothing to do with how he felt about Zoe. The feelings Zoe brought out in him were raw and a little primal. He just wanted to claim this woman, to taste every inch of her and then start all over again. She made him feel off-balance in the best way possible. Of course saying that out loud wouldn't be a smart move. She was trying to keep her distance.

He'd let her. For tonight.

But tomorrow—or later today—was a different story. They were under the same roof so he had plenty of time to prove to her that he wasn't into her for whatever bullshit reason Vincent seemed to think. The thought of using a woman that way made him sick.

He let his hands drop and nodded. "Okay."

Her dark eyes narrowed slightly. "Okay?"

"You want me to argue?"

Her lips pulled into a thin line. "No, you just have this . . . look in your eyes right now."

Sawyer raised an eyebrow. "Look?"

"It's very mischievous."

He snorted at her word choice. "Mischievous is for little boys. Something I am not," he murmured.

For a moment her eyes grew heavy-lidded as they strayed over the length of his body, down to his feet, pausing right below his belt on her upsweep, before she seemed to remember herself and focused on his face. "No, you're definitely not," she said softly.

Those words made his dick ache. Damn it, he wanted to say more. So much more, but he didn't. He knew if he pushed her right now he could get her naked and underneath him, begging for more. But he didn't want her like that, not when she was so vulnerable and not when he had to push. He wanted her to come to him.

Rubbing a hand over the back of his neck, he nodded toward the doorway. "Come on, let's get our bags and get settled in." Then he wanted to do another sweep of the house. But he didn't say that out loud since she was already nervous enough.

Unfortunately they'd be sleeping in separate rooms.

But come the morning, all bets were off. He was going to show Zoe all the reasons they should be together.

CHAPTER ELEVEN

Zoe stared at the ceiling of her room. A gauzy cano-py draped over the four-poster bed but it was sheer and she could see through it. Twinkle lights lined the head of the bed and across the back part of the canopy, but she'd unplugged them, finding them distracting.

Each time the wind whistled up over the ocean, she nearly jumped out of her skin, then wanted to curse her-self. She was in a new place, hiding from a deranged maniac and had a sexy man down the hall who'd made it very clear what he wanted from her. At least physically.

She grabbed a pillow and put it over her face, groan-ing, before tossing it off her. She could be naked and wrapped up in strong, warm arms right now. Deep down she knew she was just being a coward where Saw-yer was concerned. The man was walking, talking sex appeal, but more than that he was honorable and simply put, a good man.

If he just wanted casual he wouldn't have brought her here, protected her. Right? It didn't make sense. She guessed he could have gotten her out of the city out of a sense of duty, but that didn't feel right. Not when she had family to stay with. No, he'd gone the extra mile in a way most people wouldn't have. He'd even put off his first official week of work to bring her here. That was . . . pretty incredible. He hadn't wanted to tell her either, but she'd gotten the details out of him on the drive here.

The more she thought about him, the more elusive sleep became. She was too caught up in her own thoughts, letting her past experiences mess with her potential future. God, she really was a coward.

Rolling over, she looked at the bedside clock. It was five in the morning and she wasn't going back to sleep. Definitely time for some coffee. She doubted Sawyer would be up, not when he'd driven them to Saint Augustine and she was almost certain he'd still been up after she'd fallen asleep last night.

Wearing long, green and white striped pajama pants and a matching spaghetti strap top, she dug a cardigan out of her bag and slipped it on before leaving her room. The heat was on, but there was still a chill in the air.

The floorboards creaked beneath her when she stepped out of the room and she winced at the over-pronounced sound. A long Persian runner ran the length of the hallway and another down the wooden stairs so she kept to it so her feet wouldn't get chilled.

She'd barely taken three steps when Sawyer appeared in the doorway to his room. Her heart jumped in her throat at his sudden appearance. When she saw the gun in his hand, her eyes widened. She knew he'd brought at least one, but seeing it put her on edge. It was just a reminder of the danger she was in.

"Hold on," he murmured, before disappearing back into the darkness of his room. A second later he was back, sans gun. "Everything okay?"

"Yeah." She nodded, her gaze straying over his bare chest. He had on loose drawstring pants that she had a feeling he was only wearing because of the situation. Something told her he was a commando kind of guy.

He placed his hands on the frame and she followed the action, drinking in the lines and striations of his muscular arms. Was he doing that intentionally, trying to distract her with his sex appeal? If so, it was working. When his hands tightened suddenly, his arm muscles flexing, she met his gaze to find him watching her intently. *Hungrily.*

"Did I wake you up?" she asked, resisting the urge to wrap her arms around herself. She wasn't scared of him—never that—just a little nervous.

He shook his head, his green eyes practically smoldering. She wished he would say something. Instead he just watched her, the heat simmering there undeniable. He was making it clear what he wanted from her without saying a word.

She cleared her throat, resenting him a little for making her feel nervous and out of sorts. No one had ever had this effect on her body, not even her ex. But it was like Sawyer was just attuned to her. She had to keep her distance or else she'd never be able to resist him. "I'm going to make some coffee, do you want some?" Amazingly, her voice sounded normal, nothing like her quaking insides.

His gaze landed on her lips. "That's not what I want this morning," he murmured, his voice a lower octave than she'd ever heard.

Heat pooled low in her belly and her nipples automatically pebbled. "What do you want?" Why was she asking? She knew the answer. Some part of her desperately wanted him to say the words, to spell out exactly what he wanted. Seeing him like this, knowing he'd dropped everything in his life to help her out when he didn't have to, was one of the biggest turn-ons she could have ever imagined.

He dropped his arms and stepped out of the doorway, his prowl reminding her of a predator on a hunt. "I think you know."

"Say it," she whispered, surprising herself.

"Take off your sweater." His words were a quiet order, the demanding note behind them increasing the warmth between her legs by a hundred degrees.

Without pause, she shrugged it off, letting it fall to the ground in the hallway. What was going to happen between them—again—was a foregone conclusion. She could try to keep her distance but spending time alone with Sawyer pretty much made her lose all self-control. And she was okay with that. The payoff would be worth it if their first time together was any indication. She might be nervous about how things would play out between them but he was worth the risk.

"Now your top." His gaze was still intent on hers, those dark green eyes pinning her in place.

She was so damn slick between her legs it was almost embarrassing. He hadn't even touched her and she was ridiculously turned on. This time she did pause, just for a moment, before peeling the thin pajama top off. He'd seen her naked, but that had been fast and furious in her kitchen. She hadn't even taken her chemise all the way off, it had ended up bunched around her waist.

Now things had slowed down and it was nerve-wracking. Her top joined her sweater on the floor. Before he could give her another order, she strode past him into his room.

The drapes were pulled back but the blinds were shut, letting in very little light. She could see enough to make out the queen-sized bed and blue and white French country décor.

She hadn't made it past the threshold before he was behind her, *on* her, his big hands clutching her hips as he tugged her back flush to his torso. His skin was hot against her back. The skin on skin was too much and not enough.

He let out a soft growl as his hands slid up her hips, spanning her waist and stomach before cupping her breasts. He didn't touch her nipples though, just held her gently. She had curves but she wasn't exactly overflowing up top. Not that Sawyer seemed to mind.

Leaning down, he nipped her earlobe, his breath warm on her face. His erection pressed insistently against her back, but he seemed to be taking his time. Which was fine with her.

"I'm not walking away from this thing between us, Zoe," he whispered darkly, his words sending a shiver through her. She didn't know what to say and he surprised her by continuing. "If you're thinking of using me for sex this morning, fine. But it's not just about fucking for me."

His words sent a thrill through her. She loved the way he was so honest about everything. After dealing with a maniac who couldn't take no for an answer, who didn't understand the difference between reality and his crazy fictional world, being with someone as blunt as Sawyer was a breath of fresh air. He said what he meant and she knew that if she told him to stop, even if he was inside her, he would. No questions asked.

She trusted him implicitly. Above all, that was so freeing.

"What is it about?" The question came out as a whisper. In the mostly-darkness, with her back to him, it was easy to be brave, to say what she wanted.

He stilled behind her for a moment and she wondered if he'd respond at all. Slowly, he took her earlobe between his teeth, pressing down on the sensitive area just as his hands fully cupped her breasts, his thumbs swiping over her nipples. Too many sensations twined through her as she arched into his hold.

"I want you to remember the feel of me inside you even when I'm not with you." He dropped one hand from her breast to sweep her hair out of the way. Slowly, torturously, he kissed a hot path along the back of her neck. Her head fell forward as he teased her, both with his mouth and his hand, which gently stroked over her nipple in soft little circles.

Knees weak, she leaned back into him. His other hand snagged around her waist, pulling her tighter to him. His thick length pressed insistently against her and her inner walls clenched, unfulfilled. She desperately wanted to feel him inside her.

"It's about you trusting me," he continued, surprising her.

She'd been so caught up in how he was making her feel she'd forgotten she asked him a question. "I do."

He stilled again for a moment before he continued his slow dance of kisses, now along her shoulders. She shivered and reached back to hold him. There wasn't much she could grab other than his behind and that was fine with her. When she dug her fingers into him, he made a sexy, growling sound against her skin.

Before she knew it, he'd moved them to the bed and she was flat on her back against the tangled sheets. The second her back hit the covers, his hands were on the waist of her pajama bottoms, tugging them and her panties down. Her toes curled into the sheets as she was completely bared to him.

He still had on his drawstring pants, something she wanted to remedy soon. She reached for him, ready to push them down, but he moved lightning quick, his hands grasping her wrists.

"Shit," he murmured, his gaze hot on hers.

A small sliver of alarm twisted through her, her heart rate increasing. "What?"

He gritted his teeth. "No condoms. I fucking forgot them." Self-loathing pulsed off him.

She'd already told him she was on birth control so... "I'm clean."

Crouched above her, his big body so beautiful she wanted to stroke every inch of it, he rasped out, "Me too."

That was that. If it had been anyone else, under any other circumstances, she'd have waited to do tests but she trusted him. "Okay."

He sucked in a shallow breath and his eyes dilated, the hunger there so damn palpable she could reach out and touch it. When he looked down again, his laser-like focus narrowing between her legs, she fought the urge to squirm under that intensity. She really wanted to taste him—all of him—but it was pretty clear what he had in mind.

And she definitely wasn't going to stop him.

Reaching out, he slid a finger down her slit and let out a groan. "You're so damn wet," he murmured. In her kitchen, he'd been unsteady. Not now. Now he was in control. His jaw was clenched tight and the tendons in his neck kept flexing, telling her he was barely holding onto that control, but this was different than before. She loved it.

Slowly, gently, he slid a finger inside her and they both groaned as she tightened around him. "Fuck, Zoe. You're going to kill me."

She shifted lower against the bed, forcing him deeper inside her, her breathing erratic and unsteady. His gaze snapped to hers, a wicked grin spreading across his face before he dipped his head down between the apex of her thighs, his mouth zeroing in on her clit as if he knew exactly what she needed.

And he did.

The man apparently forgot nothing about what she liked. His tongue teased against her pulsing bundle of nerves, the rhythm of his thrusting finger perfect. Almost alarmingly so. Without warning he slid another finger inside her, her slick body welcoming him as his tongue and teeth continued stroking against her.

She slid her fingers through his short hair, her back arching off the bed as she grinded against his face and fingers. He made her feel so amazing it was hard to be self-conscious as she immediately started to build higher and higher to climax.

All her muscles pulled tight, her body tensing for what she knew was to come. It should be too soon but she'd been primed forever, just lying in bed thinking about Sawyer. The man was her walking, talking fantasy come to life.

Rough around the edges, protective, smart, sexy as hell, and didn't worry that she was some delicate flower between the sheets. He was a very unique man, one she didn't plan to let get away. She'd be insane to do that.

"Come for me," he growled against her clit. The desperateness in his voice was what pushed her over the edge.

Letting go, her orgasm punched through her, slamming into all her nerve endings as he continued teasing her clit. It finally got to the point where it bordered on painful. She tightened her grip on his head and tried to move back, but he beat her to it.

He withdrew his fingers and sat up before he quickly covered her body with his. His mouth crushed over hers, his tongue demanding entrance as he wrapped his arms around her.

She loved the feel of him covering her, his huge body one protective embrace as he rolled his hips against her, his erection rock hard. She reached between them and slid her hand down his pants. No boxers, just commando.

Groaning into his mouth, she wrapped her fingers around his thickness. He made a strangled sound and thrust into her grip, letting her stroke him up and down until finally he tore his mouth from hers.

"I want to take you from behind." His words were guttural, sexy, and he was sort of asking.

She could see that raw look in his eyes. He wanted to just flip her onto her knees and pound into her. If they'd been a couple or had been dating longer, she knew he'd have done just that. But he was holding back. Probably because he was worried about her after the crap she'd dealt with recently.

Well, he didn't need to worry. Without pause, she rolled over and pushed her ass back to him. That seemed to set him off. "Fuck," he growled, the sound raw and strained. She looked over her shoulder, watching his hands shake as he stripped off his pants.

Then he was back on the bed, one of his big hands smoothing down the length of her spine as the other guided his hard length to her entrance.

When he pushed inside her, she let her head fall forward. He filled her completely in this position, her inner walls molded around him as if they'd been made for each other. For how she felt right now, maybe they had. The man had gotten under her skin in a way no one ever had.

The chemistry was almost too much. And at the same time, not enough. She simply couldn't get enough of him, wondered if she ever would.

When he pulled back and slid into her again, she moaned his name. "Sawyer."

Her clit was pulsing, begging to be touched again. Feeling bold, she reached between her legs and started stroking herself as he began thrusting.

"Oh yeah, touch yourself, sweetheart. Come on my dick," he rasped out, his voice a bare whisper.

His words set her entire body aflame. Her breasts felt heavy, her nipples tingling, as he grabbed one of her hips. He found a delicious rhythm that had her inner walls growing tighter and tighter around him. When he reached up and cupped one of her breasts, unexpectedly tweaking her nipple between his thumb and forefinger, she cried out.

Another climax slammed into her, the pleasure more intense than before. Maybe it was because he was inside her, completely filling her, hitting that very important spot. Whatever it was, she clawed at the sheets, moving her body back to meet his with each intense thrust as she pushed over the edge.

He had to feel her coming around him, her inner walls tightening out of control as she called out his name again. Or she tried to. It was hard to think let alone speak straight. Her words were a garbled mess.

When one of his hands tightened almost painfully on her hip and he dropped his other hand from her breast, she knew he was about to let go too.

Just like that, he did, his thrusts erratic as he cried out, releasing himself inside her in long, hot streams. It seemed to go on forever as they lost themselves with each other.

As he came down from his high, he let out a protesting groan as he pulled out of her. Her inner thighs were sticky with both their juices, but she was glad when he didn't rush to grab something to clean up.

Instead, he turned her over, which was good because her limbs were useless noodles right now. Covering her face in sweet kisses, he pulled her close, his big hands sliding up and down her back and settling on her ass as he rolled onto his back, pulling her on top of him.

Spent, she laid her head on his chest, her arms loosely wrapped around his neck. She could feel his heart beat against her chest, the staccato rhythm steady, if a little faster than normal. "That was amazing," she murmured, feeling lethargic and satisfied, glad they had nowhere else to be today. Because they were definitely doing that again soon.

After a few minutes passed, he rolled his hips once, his cock already half-hard against her lower abdomen. "Feel like taking a shower with me?"

She grinned against his chest without looking up at him. "You're a monster," she muttered.

"You like it."

That was true. She should be too damn tired but . . . who was she kidding? If he was up for another round, she was taking full advantage.

CHAPTER TWELVE

She looked around the grocery store parking lot, making sure no one was paying any attention to her before turning her attention back to Zoe and her new lover. She'd tracked Zoe to Saint Augustine, right down to the beach house she was staying at. It had been so easy, tracking Zoe. All she'd had to do was use the ADM—android device manager—linked to Zoe's phone. It was Zoe's own fault for being so stupid, for leaving her email open at work and giving anyone access to her personal information. After that, now she could track Zoe anywhere as long as she had her phone on her and turned on since all her accounts were synced.

So far she hadn't been able to properly scout the house without getting caught because the street was a dead end and the houses were so far apart she'd be spotted easily if someone looked out a window. She could have gone jogging down the street, but she hadn't wanted to risk being recognized. Not when she'd come so far.

Instead she'd parked at a gas station at the end of the road where the house was—and waited. It'd been long and tedious to just wait but she didn't mind being patient. And making sure Zoe paid for all she'd done was worth sitting in her car all day. She wasn't going to drag this out much longer, not when she had more pressing matters to deal with back home.

With Zoe out of town, she could kill two birds with one stone. Eliminate Zoe and focus on her next love interest. Now that Braddock was dead she needed someone else to fill her bed. Someone better than him. Someone kind and not so narcissistic. While Braddock had had many wonderful attributes, what with being a renowned surgeon and so wealthy, he'd lacked so much emotionally. Her next lover wouldn't be like that. No, he'd be happy to have someone like her in his life. But only if Zoe was gone.

Now it appeared she'd have the chance to get rid of her sooner than she'd hoped. Just as she'd been about to head back to her motel, she'd seen Zoe's male friend pulling out onto the street. Now the bitch and he were at a grocery store. Instead of following them inside, even though she desperately wanted to get a peek at Zoe's face, to see if she was stressed or scared, she wasn't going to pass up this opportunity.

She knew exactly where they were, and would have a limited time to check out the exterior of the house and come up with a game plan. Well, she didn't have to decide now. Steering out of the parking lot, she could barely contain the thrill that punched through her.

Soon justice would be done. Zoe would be gone forever. She just needed to decide how she was going to kill Zoe. She'd played out too many fantasies in her head. The one thing she was certain of, she'd have to shoot Zoe's lover. Maybe not kill him first though. A gut shot so he'd bleed out while Zoe watched. Maybe even make it look like Zoe had killed him then killed herself.

That thought brought on a rush of pleasure. She'd have to make sure she cleaned up all her DNA if she did that, make it appear as if she'd never been there. Once she scouted the house, she'd be able to figure out her exact plan better.

The only thing certain right now was that Zoe was going to die, but she'd watch her friend go first.

* * *

Sawyer looked out the glass sliding door leading to the lower back deck, a frown tugging at his mouth. The sun was now setting and ever since they'd left the grocery store that morning, he hadn't been able to shake an uneasy feeling. Not the kind where someone was looking at him through a sniper scope, but the kind where something bad was on the horizon.

He could just chalk it up to the whole situation of being in hiding, but something tickled his senses.

"You look way too tense," Zoe murmured, her arms coming around him from behind as she laid her head on his back.

He covered her arms with his own, linking his fingers through hers. She'd been impressive today, not complaining once that they hadn't been able to leave except to get groceries. Not that he'd expected her to, but he knew how civilians could be, especially after his last month of training for Red Stone Security. People didn't like feeling as if they were caged, even if the surroundings were nice, and it could make them react poorly. Not Zoe. "Sorry we couldn't hit the beach today."

She laughed lightly against his back. "Stop apologizing for protecting me. Besides it's cold outside and I've had a lot of fun in here with you." Her voice took on a seductive quality, her grip around him tightening.

Grinning, he reached up and pulled the curtains into place over the door before turning to pull Zoe into his arms. They'd definitely found ways to occupy their time. He'd already fallen hard for this woman. The sex was part of it; their chemistry undeniable, but it was more. Way more. Once they returned to Miami he wanted something serious with her. Hell, he wanted serious right now. "So what did your brother and mom say?" She'd gone up to her room—which he was now sharing with her—to call her family.

"Vincent wants me to come home but my mom's glad I'm here with you. She likes you a lot." Zoe paused, watching him carefully, as if debating something.

He liked her mom too but decided not to respond when it was clear she wanted to say more. He'd noticed that she did that sometimes, was silent while she gathered her thoughts. When she didn't continue, he chose to break the silence, tightening his arms around her waist. "What is it?"

Zoe bit her full bottom lip, her dark eyes filled with too many complex emotions for him to sift through. One of her hands was on his hip but she placed the other on his chest. "You don't have to say yes, but . . . if it's safe enough by then, my mom wanted to invite you over for Christmas dinner. But only if you don't have plans, don't feel obligated or anything," she rushed to add.

Her invitation warmed him, telling him she really did want him in her life. Not just physically. The invitation might have come from her mom, but Zoe wouldn't have mentioned it if she didn't want him there. Still, he wanted her to ask. "Your mom invited me? What about you, do you want me there?"

Her cheeks flushed red. "What do you think?"

"I think I want to hear you say the words."

"You are maddening," she muttered, a grin pulling at her lips. "Fine, I would like to invite you over for Christmas dinner—and Christmas Eve. It's not a big deal, but on Christmas Eve we all get together to open one present and play dirty Santa." For just a moment, a raw vulnerability bled into her gaze before she quickly covered it.

"I'd love to," he murmured, dropping a soft kiss on her lips. He hadn't planned to go home this year because it would have been too much travel after just starting a new job, but especially not now when things with Zoe's stalker were still up in the air. Sawyer had spoken to Carlito a couple hours ago and they were still running down leads. He knew they couldn't hide out forever and would have to head back to Miami for Christmas no matter if the guy was caught or not.

Her eyes lit up for a second, but then she frowned. "You're sure? I don't want you to feel pressured."

"*Zoe*," he rasped out before crushing his mouth over hers in a swift, claiming kiss. Though he hated to, he pulled back, his heart rate already kicking up at the simple taste of her. "I don't feel pressured. I want to date you—and only you." While his experience with real relationships was limited, he figured he needed to make this clear since it apparently wasn't.

She watched him for a long moment, her beautiful eyes unreadable. Finally she pressed against his chest. "I've got hot chocolate in the kitchen—instant, so don't get too excited," she said, a smile tugging at her lips before her expression turned serious. "Let's drink it while it's hot and . . . I need to tell you something."

His gut clenched at her words and worried expression. He told her that he wanted to date only her and her response was that she wanted to tell him something over instant hot chocolate. That did not sound promising. "Okay."

Once in the big kitchen she took a seat at the center island, waiting for him to join her before she picked up her mug. "I didn't know if you wanted marshmallows," she said, nodding at the open bag. He noticed she'd added a ton to hers.

"Thanks." He tossed some in, letting them melt while he waited for her to say whatever it was she needed to get off her chest. He just hoped it wasn't that she didn't want to see him, because he wasn't sure how he'd deal with that.

"I've only had one serious relationship, which is probably pretty sad, but there it is. I was with Rubin for a couple years. We had a lot in common and . . . Well, that's not important." Her cheeks flushed slightly as she continued. "We were serious and heading for marriage. Or, I mistakenly thought we were. The day after we graduated from med school, he..." She swallowed hard, but didn't take her gaze from Sawyer. "He ended things because he was getting back together with his ex. He said he'd wanted to wait until after exams to end things because he didn't want to affect my finals—which was actually really nice of him. The thing is, he was a decent guy. I wish I could talk trash about him and say how awful he was, but . . . I guess what I'm trying to say is I had the perfect guy on paper and it didn't work out because I wasn't enough—"

"Bullshit," Sawyer snapped out.

Her eyes widened. "What?"

"The fact that you didn't work out with him isn't because you weren't enough." He scowled, the very thought pissing him off.

"Well, whatever the reason, we didn't work out because he was still hung up on his ex. I really like you, Sawyer." God he loved it when she said his name. "I'm falling for you faster than I imagined possible to fall for anyone and, I just…" She trailed off and it took him a few seconds to understand what she was saying—or wasn't saying.

Hoping he wasn't completely in left field with his assumption, he took her free hand in his. "I'm not still hung up on Audrey." Even saying her name after so long felt odd. He hadn't thought about her in years. Zoe stiffened slightly but didn't pull away and for that he was glad. "I loved her, or thought I did. Back then all I did was travel and as crass as it sounds, she was someone to come home to." Things had been purely physical between them, he just hadn't been able to tell the difference, something he didn't think Zoe needed to hear right now.

"I was in a different place then, gone out of the country more often than not and . . . if you're worried that I'm settling or that you're second to *anyone*, that's insane. What I feel for you is different than anything I've ever felt before. I can see a future with us." Putting that out there made him feel so damn exposed but he needed her to know, to understand.

She pushed out a long breath, as if she'd been holding it, before a real smile broke out over her face. The kind that made his entire body react. "I can too."

Thank God. "Since we're in confession mode, you should know that I followed you yesterday. After you told me to leave and ran your errands . . . I was fucking worried and tailed you to make sure no one else was watching you. Once you made it to your street, I headed home." Now he wished he'd just followed her all the way to her driveway considering the 'present' she'd been left on her doorstep. "After what you've been through, I just want it out there."

Her eyebrows raised a fraction. "You followed me to the salon and everywhere else?"

He nodded.

She let out a short laugh. "I think I'm more embarrassed than anything that I didn't even notice."

"If you had noticed then I need to find a new job," he murmured, thankful she didn't seem angry at him.

Shaking her head, she smiled then leaned closer to him. His whole body tightened as he moved in to cover the distance between them. His cell phone rang, making them both pause. Zoe let out a soft groan and sat back in her seat, plucking her hot chocolate from the counter. "You better see who it is."

Even though he didn't want to, he pulled his phone from his pants pocket. When he saw Detective Duarte's name on the caller ID, he answered immediately. "Yeah?"

Zoe straightened, watching him carefully.

Carlito's voice came through crystal clear. "Everything's fine, just calling to check on you guys and to let you know I've put in a call to the Saint Augustine PD to let them know what's going on and to give them your address. If you see a patrol car drive by more than once tonight, that's why."

Sawyer's eyebrows raised in surprise. "Thanks. I'll let Zoe know. Any news?"

The other man sighed. "Nothing solid. Klein's wife gave me a list of possible women her ex either had an affair with or was possibly still having one with. She hadn't talked to him in months and isn't sure he was sleeping with all of them, but she had her suspicions. It's pretty extensive for one guy." He sounded disgusted.

"You want Zoe to look at it?" Maybe she knew one or more of the women, which might not mean anything at all, but it could be a help if there was some connection to Zoe and Klein that intersected somewhere.

"Yeah, I've just emailed it to her but wanted to give you guys a head's up in case she wasn't checking often. You sure you guys are doing good?"

"Yeah, locked down tight. Security system's top of the line and I'm armed."

After a few more minutes of small talk, they disconnected and he relayed the message to Zoe.

She slid off her seat, barely concealed hope in her eyes. "I'm going to grab my phone and check my email."

"I'll head up with you. Once you've read it, we can use the hot tub on the upper deck." Because even if someone was using a high-powered rifle with night vision—from a boat on the ocean—they were still safe on the upper deck. He'd already scouted it out and the layout gave them privacy from the beach. His brother had had the house built that way, so they could still use the hot tub in the winter and be blocked from the ocean wind. Of course the two heaters in the hot tub alcove would keep them warm too.

Her eyes glinted with lust as she nodded. "Sounds like a plan to me."

He might hate that the situation was so bad Zoe was forced into hiding, but he was glad things between them had moved so fast. He didn't plan on slowing down either. He wanted everything from Zoe and convincing her that he was in this for the long-term was going to involve a lot of naked time together if he had anything to say about it.

CHAPTER THIRTEEN

Zoe slid into the hot tub, embracing the heat as it enveloped her. Sawyer had been right, this was a great idea. The alarm on the house was set and unless someone used a grappling hook, they weren't getting to the upper deck. Even though it was on the second floor, it was technically three stories up because the first level was on stilts so she wasn't worried about someone climbing up to attack them.

Since Sawyer wasn't either, she was letting herself relax. As much as she could anyway. The day spent with Sawyer had been therapeutic.

"What are you thinking?" Sawyer asked, stepping into the water and sitting next to her. He'd slid his gun under one of the towels, keeping it close just in case.

Which was fine with her. She shifted and turned sideways, putting her feet in his lap, thinking that they would be naked in a few minutes. She wasn't even sure why they'd bothered with bathing suits. "That this is a weird kind of vacation but there's nowhere else I want to be right now."

He gave her one of those boyish grins that made butterflies take off inside her. Sawyer was all man, with a rugged face, sharp lines and striations showcasing all his muscles, but sometimes when he smiled he looked a decade younger. The man was sexy and adorable at the same time. "I agree."

"You sure you're not going to get in trouble at work for this?" She held up her hands when he frowned, his expression darkening. He'd already reassured her, but she still felt bad that she'd pulled him away from a new job. "I'm just making sure. Taking a management position with Red Stone is a big deal."

He sighed but nodded. "Trust me, it's fine. I explained everything to Porter Caldwell and he was more than happy to let me off to help you."

"Happy?" Zoe had met all the Caldwell brothers and they were pretty intense. So was Sawyer, but still, she couldn't imagine Porter being 'happy' to let Sawyer take time off so soon after starting.

Sawyer nodded. "Apparently you helped out Red Stone not too long ago when one of their agents was kidnapped. Got them access to the hospital's security feeds without involving law enforcement?"

"Oh, right." She hadn't forgotten, but she hadn't realized Porter Caldwell had known about it. Though she should have. "I had to go on a date with someone for that," she muttered, remembering how annoyed she'd been at the time. And relieved when everything had worked out.

Sawyer laughed. "I take it everything ended up okay?"

She nodded. "Yep. The woman doesn't work for Red Stone anymore and as far as I know, she actually freed herself from the kidnapper, but things definitely worked out since she's now blissfully married to an honest to goodness billionaire." Her brother had gone to their wedding over the summer.

Sawyer let out a low whistle.

"I know, right?"

Sawyer started massaging one of her feet, his knuckles rubbing over her arch, his eyes going heavy-lidded as he watched her. "So, you don't mind breaking the rules just a little bit, huh?"

Grinning, she started to answer when Sawyer stilled and dropped her foot. He turned, going for his gun when she heard, then *saw* the problem.

Viola was standing in the doorway to the bedroom, a gun pointed directly at Sawyer's chest.

Zoe's heart felt as if it stopped as she watched the other woman step out onto the deck, her normally sleek black hair a tangled mess around her pretty face. Her blue eyes were glassy and her black jacket and jogging pants were shredded in places. *What. The. Hell.*

"Don't move a muscle!" Viola snapped, her hands shaking. She couldn't know Sawyer had a weapon hidden, or Zoe didn't think the woman did.

174 | KATIE REUS

Zoe felt frozen, unable to look away from the barrel of the gun. As a surgeon, she'd seen firsthand exactly how deadly they could be, what a bullet could do to someone's insides. And right now a maniac was pointing one at the man she'd fallen for. Her stomach roiled.

"No one's moving," Sawyer said, his voice incredibly calm.

That was what tugged Zoe out of her frozen state. She cleared her throat and focused on Viola's rage-filled face. "Viola, what's going on?" Somehow, her voice didn't shake.

The woman's gaze and weapon trained on Zoe. "It's all your fault he's dead!"

Next to her Sawyer stiffened a fraction, but he didn't make any sudden moves. Zoe swallowed hard, trying to remain calm. "Who is dead?"

"Braddock, you idiot." Her voice and hands shook again, making Zoe tense.

"I didn't kill him."

Viola's jaw clenched. "I know that. I did, but it's your fault. He was happy with me, had even left his wife, but the second he strolls back into town he had to see you. It was always about you," she spat, her eyes glittering with surprising tears.

Zoe stared at the woman in confusion and terror. It sounded a lot like her stalker had had a stalker of his own. And Viola was clearly certifiable. Zoe was terrified but knew she needed to keep Viola talking, anything to keep the woman focused on her and not Sawyer. "Why did you get a job at Gerard's practice?" Because Viola had started working there after Zoe had. That couldn't be a coincidence.

Next to Zoe, Sawyer shifted a fraction. It was subtle, the movement barely discernible over the bubbles of the jets.

Her blue eyes narrowed angrily. "To keep an eye on you. I knew you were after Braddock but I thought maybe you'd moved on when you quit at the hospital, when you realized you couldn't have him. That he was *mine*."

Zoe forced her expression to remain bland, not to reveal her 'what the hell' face to Viola. That was when it hit her. What she'd just read in that email from Carlito. "Your first name is Courtney." There had been a Courtney *V* Rice in the list of names Detective Duarte had sent her. Viola Rice. It was too much of a coincidence that a woman with the same last name of Rice was on that list. Zoe wished she'd figured that out sooner, but it probably wouldn't have done her any good because Viola had somehow gotten into this house past the security system undetected. Zoe couldn't figure out how.

When Viola didn't respond, Zoe continued. "Do you need medical help?" Zoe motioned to the scrapes and cuts visible where her clothes were ripped. Had she gotten cut with glass?

Viola snorted. "Don't act like you care. Get up. Both of you!" She whipped her gaze to Sawyer, but kept the weapon trained on Zoe.

A surreal iciness filled Zoe's veins as she looked at Sawyer. He nodded and slowly stood with her.

"What do you plan to do with us?" Sawyer asked, his movements glacially slow as he stepped onto where he'd been sitting.

Zoe couldn't tell if he was going to go for the weapon or if he was just moving slowly because he didn't want to startle Viola.

"Maybe a murder-suicide." She laughed, the eerie sound bouncing off the walls of the small alcove, the wind whistling over the ocean creepy background music.

"No one will ever believe that," Zoe said, stepping up onto the seat too.

"And you're never going to do anything with the safety on," Sawyer said, derision in his voice.

Viola frowned and turned the gun to the side to inspect it. That was all the distraction Sawyer needed.

Everything seemed to happen in slow motion as he dove for the towel covering his gun. Instinct kicked in as Zoe jumped in the opposite direction over the hot tub ledge. Staying separated would make it harder for Viola to shoot them both.

Viola screamed and swiveled toward Zoe, gun raised. There was nowhere to go.

Pop. Pop. Pop.

Bracing for the pain, Zoe cringed, all the muscles in her body pulling taut as she landed on the wooden deck with a thud. Viola just stood there, staring eerily at Zoe.

Her heart beat out of control. Had she been shot? Too stunned to move, she flinched when the gun tumbled from Viola's fingers, rolling along the ground before hitting the water with a splash. That was when Zoe saw the hole in the woman's forehead. Eyes wide but not seeing anything, Viola fell to her knees before falling onto her face. The other two shots she'd heard must have hit her in the chest, but it was impossible to tell with all that black clothing.

Just like that, the slow motion seemed to speed up like a video fast-forwarding.

"Zoe!" Sawyer was around the big hot tub before Zoe had fully stood, gathering her into his arms. He held her shoulders and raked a gaze over her body from head to toe, inspecting her for a wound that wasn't there.

She had a dozen questions, like how the hell that maniac had gotten into the house or even found them, but she didn't care about *any* of them right now. Sawyer was alive and so was she. If only she could stop shaking. Her teeth chattered out of control and she was vaguely aware that shock was seeping into her system.

Oh, God. They'd almost died. If it hadn't been for Sawyer, she'd definitely be dead. Sobbing, she buried her face against his chest, letting him comfort her as she soaked up all his strength. Her nightmare was over.

CHAPTER FOURTEEN

One week later

Sawyer glanced up from snagging one of Tanice's sugar cookies, then paused when he saw Vincent entering the kitchen. Tension seemed to follow, but Sawyer just ignored it.

Zoe had sent him into the kitchen to grab another bottle of champagne and it had been impossible not to eat another cookie before leaving. She might hate to cook but her mom sure could—and had promised him years of home cooked meals. As if he needed a reason to stay with Zoe. He nearly snorted at the thought.

Vincent opened the refrigerator and grabbed another bottle of champagne, but kept his gaze on Sawyer. "I think we're going to need two."

Sawyer nodded. Things were still awkward between him and Vincent but after he'd saved Zoe's life the other man had seemed to realize he wasn't going anywhere. Which was good, because he wasn't and he didn't want strife with his future brother-in-law. Not that he'd actually asked Zoe to marry him yet, or even told her he loved her, but it was coming. He felt it in his bones.

Vincent shut the door but didn't make a move to leave the room. "Listen, I was a dick—back in California and at Zoe's house—and I'm fucking sorry."

"Your mom make you apologize?"

Vincent let out a bark of laughter and shook his head. "No, but she would if she knew what I'd done." He scrubbed a hand over his buzzed hair. "Seriously, man, I really am sorry. It's obvious Zoe cares about you or she'd have never brought you to meet the family and I just want her to be happy."

"I do too." More than his next breath.

"Yeah, I kinda figured that." He paused, watching Sawyer intently. "So how serious are you two?"

Sawyer picked up the champagne bottle he'd left on the counter and two cookies for good measure. He didn't need to tell Vincent anything, but he was Zoe's brother and despite their history, a good man at his core. Besides, as a fellow SEAL, even if they hadn't been in the same class, they'd always be part of the same brotherhood. And Sawyer didn't want any tension between them so he went for honesty. "I don't know about her, but she's it for me." Though he hoped she felt the same way about him.

After what had happened in Saint Augustine, he was grateful to be able to hold Zoe in his arms, to see her every day. The fact that a woman had managed to break into the beach house—using a small, high stained-glass window from one of the downstairs guest bathrooms as her point of entrance—still gave him nightmares. He'd checked the entire house multiple times and he'd known that window hadn't been linked to the security system—because no one should have been able to get through the damn thing. But Viola Rice had clawed her way through it, not caring that she'd sliced herself up to get to Zoe. And the police had eventually figured out that she'd tracked Zoe using a locator program on her phone. Fucking technology.

Vincent's eyebrows raised the slightest fraction then he nodded once, as if in agreement. "Good."

Zoe strode into the kitchen then, looking gorgeous in a red and gold dress that accentuated all her curves. Without pause she moved into Sawyer's side, wrapping her arm around his waist as he slid his arm around her shoulders. She narrowed her eyes at Vincent. "You giving my man a hard time?"

"We're bonding."

She snorted and swatted at him. "Well you better get in there, it's almost dirty Santa time."

As soon as Vincent had left, Zoe turned into Sawyer's embrace and lifted up on her toes. "Was he bothering you?" Her expression was fierce and loving—and he loved that she actually worried about him, even if he didn't need it. He couldn't remember the last time anyone other than his parents had done that.

"No . . ." He ran his fingertips down the side of her cheek. "I love you, Zoe," he blurted, not wanting another second to pass before he told her. He didn't care how soon it was or that they hadn't known each other that long. For the past twenty years he'd made life and death decisions on a daily basis and he didn't often second guess himself. And he wasn't going to start now. He loved this woman more than he'd ever loved anyone and he wanted her to know.

Zoe's bright smile nearly blinded him. "I love you too." Pulling a sprig of mistletoe from behind her back she held it over her head, her grin turning playful. "Now get down here and kiss me."

Relief slammed into him at her words. He'd thought she felt the same as him, but to hear her words—it was the best Christmas present he'd ever received. He hadn't realized he'd been worried what her response would be, but hearing her say she loved him too nearly brought him to his knees. Covering her mouth with his, he knew his life was never going to be the same now that Zoe was in it. Until her he hadn't realized anything had been missing but now that she was in it, he was never letting her go.

EPILOGUE

Two months later

Laughing, Zoe collapsed into Sawyer's arms, using him for support. After dancing the last hour in high heels, she was pretty much done. "I need a drink and to rest."

"I thought you'd never ask," he murmured, ushering them off the dance floor, his big hand placed firmly at the small of her back in a proprietary manner she absolutely loved.

It took a while to make it to one of the open bars because the reception after Vincent and Jordan's wedding was packed.

Zoe had known it was going to be big, but she hadn't realized just how crowded it would be. They'd decided to do an outside wedding at a place right on the water. Twinkle lights were strung up everywhere, the sparkly atmosphere exactly what Jordan had wanted. Even though it was the tail end of winter, it was Florida and the weather was already moving into spring. The entire night had been perfect, something both her brother and Jordan deserved. Now that the newly married couple had left the reception to head out on their honeymoon, Zoe was ready to leave and get some alone time with Sawyer.

For the last two months, they'd spent pretty much every second they could together. Since they both worked a lot, it wasn't as much as she'd like so when he'd asked her to move in with him—two and a half weeks after they'd returned from Saint Augustine—she hadn't had to think about her answer. Coming home to him every night was a kind of perfection she was still trying to adjust to. Part of her was worried she'd wake up and realize all this wasn't real. But she knew it was.

"What's going on in that pretty head of yours?" Sawyer murmured, picking up two champagne glasses for them.

Just like always, her entire body flared to life as his voice rolled over her. "That I'm blessed to have found you," she said, taking one of the glasses.

He gave her one of those unreadable looks before he tilted his head in the direction of a pavilion right on the water. "Walk with me?"

Nodding, she fell in step with him, unsurprised when he slid his jacket around her shoulders. She wasn't even that cold, but he hadn't missed her slight shiver. Because he never missed a thing. "You're going to spoil me."

"Good." As they stepped up into the pavilion, an icy wind blew up over the Atlantic.

She handed him her glass and slid her hands into the sleeves, wrapping her arms around herself. Okay, maybe it was colder than she'd thought. As she tucked her hands into the pockets her fingers touched a small box.

At the same moment, Sawyer got a deer-in-headlights look. It took her all of two seconds to figure out why. Or at least make an educated guess.

Surprising her, he sighed and pulled her close, his big hands resting on her hips possessively. "Pull it out," he said, almost resignedly.

With trembling fingers she did, her eyes widening when she saw a small red box. She supposed it could be earrings but... "What is this?" she whispered, her gaze fixed on his.

He swallowed hard, the vulnerable side of him he so rarely showed shining through for a fraction of a moment. "I wasn't going to do this here, but..." He took it from her hands and got down on one knee. When he opened the box to reveal a marquis cut diamond engagement ring, her breath caught in her throat. "Marry me, Zoe."

Tears blurred her vision as she nodded. "Yes," she rasped out, glad she'd managed to find her voice. Like there was a doubt what her answer would be. It had happened way sooner than she'd expected but surprisingly there was no hesitation in her. Sawyer was one of a kind and he was all hers.

She loved him more than she'd ever thought possible. He was a strong, honorable man and she couldn't wait to spend the rest of her life learning everything about him.

Thank you for reading Deadly Fallout. I really hope you enjoyed it and that you'll consider leaving a review at one of your favorite online retailers.

If you would like to read more, turn the page for a sneak peek of Bound to Danger, the second book in my Deadly Ops series and Under His Protection, a book in the Red Stone Security Series. And if you don't want to miss any future releases, please feel free to join my newsletter. I only send out a newsletter for new releases or sales news. Find the signup link on my website: http://www.katiereus.com

BOUND TO DANGER

Deadly Ops Series
Copyright © 2014 Katie Reus

Forcing her body to obey her when all she wanted to do was curl into a ball and cry until she passed out, she got up. Cool air rushed over her exposed back and backside as her feet hit the chilly linoleum floor. She wasn't wearing any panties and the hospital gown wasn't covering much of her. She didn't care.

Right now she didn't care about much at all.

Sometime when she'd been asleep her dirty, rumpled gown had been removed from the room. And someone had left a small bag of clothes on the bench by the window. No doubt Nash had brought her something to wear. He'd been in to see her a few times, but she'd asked him to leave each time. She felt like a complete bitch because she knew he just wanted to help, but she didn't care. Nothing could help, and being alone with her pain was the only way she could cope right now.

Feeling as if she were a hundred years old, she'd started unzipping the small brown leather bag when the door opened. As she turned to look over her shoulder, she found Nash, a uniformed police officer, and another really tall, thuggish-looking man entering.

Her eyes widened in recognition. The tattoos were new, but the *thug* was Cade O'Reilly. He'd served in the Marines with her brother. They'd been best friends and her brother, Riel, named after her father, had even brought him home a few times. But that was years ago. Eight to be exact. It was hard to forget the man who'd completely cut her out of his life after her brother died, as if she meant nothing to him.

Cade towered over Nash—who was pretty tall himself—and had a sleeve of tattoos on one arm and a couple on the other. His jet-black hair was almost shaved, the skull trim close to his head, just like the last time she'd seen him. He was . . . intimidating. Always had been. And startlingly handsome in that bad-boy way she was sure had made plenty of women . . . Yeah, she wasn't even going there.

She swiveled quickly, putting her back to the window so she wasn't flashing them. Reaching around to her back, she clasped the hospital gown together. "You can't knock?" she practically shouted, her voice raspy from crying, not sure whom she was directing the question to.

"I told them you weren't to be bothered, but—"

The police officer cut Nash off, his gaze kind but direct. "Ms. Cervantes, this man is from the NSA and needs to ask you some questions. As soon as you're done, the doctors will release you."

"I know who he is." She bit the words out angrily, earning a surprised look from Nash and a controlled look from Cade.

She might know Cade, or she had at one time, but she hadn't known he worked for the NSA. After her brother's death he'd stopped communicating with her.

Her brother had brought him home during one of their short leaves, and she and Cade had become friends. *Good friends.* They'd e-mailed all the time, for almost a year straight. Right near the end of their long correspondence, things had shifted between them, had been heading into more than friendly territory. Then after Riel died, it was as if Cade had too. It had cut her so deep to lose him on top of her brother. And now he showed up in the hospital room after her mom's death and wanted to talk to her? Hell no.

She'd been harassing the nurses to find a doctor who would discharge her, and now she knew why they'd been putting her off. They'd done a dozen tests and she didn't have a brain injury. She wasn't exhibiting any signs of having a concussion except for the memory loss, but the doctors were convinced that this was because of shock and trauma at what she'd apparently witnessed.

Nash started to argue, but the cop hauled him away, talking in low undertones, shutting the door behind them. Leaving her alone with this giant of a man.

Feeling raw and vulnerable, Maria wrapped her arms around herself. The sun had almost set, so even standing by the window didn't warm her up. She just felt so damn cold. Because of the room and probably grief. And now to be faced with a dark reminder of her past was too much.

UNDER HIS PROTECTION

Red Stone Security Series
Copyright © 2014 Katie Reus

"You are going to love what I got her," Julieta whispered to Lizzy.

They were sitting next to each other at Mina's bridal shower. Mina Hollingsworth, soon-to-be Mina Blue. The sweet artist was marrying former pro-football player/former Marine Alexander Blue and she was one of the nicest people Julieta had ever met.

"I take it you went off the registry," Lizzy whispered back before taking a sip of her mimosa.

"Just a bit." She held back her grin as Mina picked up her next gift. The black and white damask bag with a bright pink stripe across the top was distinctively from Julieta's store.

"I know who this is from," Mina said, already blushing as she delicately pulled the paper stuffing out the top. Her face split into a wide smile as she pulled out the sheer white, delicate lace lingerie babydoll halter. The back had ruffled layers to create a small bustle and above that in bright pink hand-done stitching were the words 'property of Alex'. Mina's fiancé might have mentioned something to Julieta about this.

As Mina pulled it out and saw the back she started laughing, her cheeks flushing an even darker shade of pink. "Did Alex ask you to do this?" she asked.

Julieta just shrugged and pursed her lips together as she fought a smile.

Mina turned it around for the twenty other women to see. Everyone started howling and talking about how much their significant others would want them to get one. Julieta ignored the small pang in her chest. For a bridal shower this one was very small and considering how wealthy Mina was, she was surprised it wasn't bigger. But maybe she shouldn't be. The woman was incredibly picky about who she was friends with—because she wasn't sure who she could trust—and she had guards around her most of the time. All the women at the shower were either married or engaged, except two of Mina's friends from California.

Being single had never bothered Julieta before. The last three years she'd been working like mad to get her business off the ground and now that it had and she was doing well, she had more time on her hands. She had a lot of friends and a huge, loving family but the truth was, she was lonely. When she'd first started her business she'd actually had a serious boyfriend. They'd been together the last two years of college, but once she'd started working long hours he'd decided he couldn't handle it. He'd said he wanted her to be successful and would support her, but in the end it had all been lip service. She was glad she'd found out before they'd taken the next step, but it still stung when she thought about how badly things had ended between them.

She couldn't remember the last date she'd gone on and unfortunately the last two months she'd spent fantasizing about a certain sexy Red Stone Security employee she kept seeing because of her friendship with Mina. But she couldn't get a read on the man. He was always so tight-lipped and gave brooding stares when she was around. She was pretty sure he didn't even like her. Not to mention Mina had mentioned that he was a total player on more than one occasion.

Which made her fantasies even more ridiculous. She wasn't into playboys or bad boys. So why did everything about Ivan make her wake up and take notice?

"Is that from your new line?" Lizzy demanded, shifting against the loveseat in the expansive living room that overlooked the Miami bay as Mina told everyone to go grab food and drinks.

Huge windows and a bright October day made for a gorgeous view and natural lighting as the women broke up and started to eat and mingle.

"Minus the personalized stitching, yes. And yes, I've already saved one for you. I can't believe you had a baby five months ago. You look amazing," she said in mock disgust.

"Porter keeps me busy." Lizzy's smile turned mischievous which only made that pang in Julieta's chest expand.

She shoved down those feelings as best she could. "Seriously, do you need to remind me how long it's been since I've had sex..." She trailed off as Ivan appeared from out of nowhere.

Wearing his standard dark suit he looked imposing and too sexy for his own good. She gritted her teeth at his timing because she was pretty sure he'd heard her. He so did not need to know she had no sex life. He nodded at both of them politely. For a brief moment she thought he'd approached to speak to her and her heart rate increased by about a thousand percent. That lasted for all of two seconds. The thought of him approaching her just to chat was as ridiculous as her fantasies about him.

"Hey Ivan, where've you been hiding?" Lizzy asked casually.

Since they both worked for Red Stone, though in different capacities, the two were friends. It shouldn't make Julieta jealous that Lizzy, one of her oldest, happily married friends, was so comfortable with Ivan. But it kind of did.

ACKNOWLEDGMENTS

Once again it's time to thank the normal crowd. Per usual, I owe a big thanks to Kari Walker! I'd be lost without you. Carolyn Crane, thank you for your character insight and fabulous attention to detail. Joan Turner, thank you for catching all those final, pesky little errors. For my readers, thank you for reading and supporting this series! Jaycee with Sweet 'N Spicy Designs, ten covers in and I love this one just as much as the others. Without a wonderfully supportive husband I wouldn't get to write as much as I do, so thank you for putting up with my schedule. For my sister, thank you for those daily phone calls that keep me sane. And as always, I owe thanks to God.

Shattered Duty

Non-series Romantic Suspense
Running From the Past
Everything to Lose
Dangerous Deception
Dangerous Secrets
Killer Secrets
Deadly Obsession
Danger in Paradise
His Secret Past

Paranormal Romance
Destined Mate
Protector's Mate
A Jaguar's Kiss
Tempting the Jaguar
Enemy Mine
Heart of the Jaguar

Moon Shifter Series
Alpha Instinct
Lover's Instinct (novella)
Primal Possession
Mating Instinct
His Untamed Desire (novella)
Avenger's Heat
Hunter Reborn

Darkness Series
Darkness Awakened
Taste of Darkness

ABOUT THE AUTHOR

Katie Reus is the *New York Times* and *USA Today* bestselling author of the Red Stone Security series, the Moon Shifter series and the Deadly Ops series. She fell in love with romance at a young age thanks to books she pilfered from her mom's stash. Years later she loves reading romance almost as much as she loves writing it.

However, she didn't always know she wanted to be a writer. After changing majors many times, she finally graduated summa cum laude with a degree in psychology. Not long after that she discovered a new love. Writing. She now spends her days writing dark paranormal romance and sexy romantic suspense.

For more information on Katie please visit her website: www.katiereus.com. Also find her on twitter @katiereus or visit her on facebook at: www.facebook.com/katiereusauthor.

50038836R00124

Made in the USA
Lexington, KY
25 August 2019